SOUL CATCHER

A John Decker Thriller Prequel

ALSO BY ANTHONY M. STRONG

THE JOHN DECKER THRILLER SERIES

What Vengeance Comes

Cold Sanctuary

Crimson Deep

Grendel's Labyrinth

Whitechapel Rising

Black Tide

Ghost Canyon

Cryptid Quest

Last Resort

JOHN DECKER SERIES PREQUEL

Soul Catcher

THE REMNANTS SERIES

The Remnants of Yesterday

The Silence of Tomorrow

STANDALONE BOOKS

The Haunting of Willow House

Crow Song

Anthony M. Strong

SOUL CATCHER

A John Decker Thriller Prequel

WEST STREET

West Street Publishing

Cover art and interior design by Bad Dog Media, LLC.
Cover Copyright Anthony M. Strong

ISBN: 978-1942207078

10 9 8 7 6 5 4 3 2

For Sonya - who scares easily

ONE

CAIRO, EGYPT

THE CITY STRETCHED in all directions, a sparkling jewel under the cloak of night, with the serpentine weave of the Nile River a thin ribbon dividing the east and west banks. The water was alive with lights, red and blue, green and white, shimmering reflections of the thousands of structures crowding the city center, each one jostling for space in the tight and noisy metropolis. One such building, the Egyptian Museum of Antiquities, sat serene and majestic, steps from the river, between Nile Corniche Street and Meret Basha, its red block façade illuminated by upward facing spotlights arranged around the walls so that it glowed as if from an ethereal light.

Inside, a portico with four pillars opened onto the central atrium, a massive space flanked by galleries on two levels and filled with wonders of the ancient world. Sarcophagi and display cases bursting with priceless artifacts lay under the watchful eyes of Amenhotep III and his queen, Tiye, immortalized in stone at the far end of the room.

Through this space, ignoring the colossal double statues, hurried a diminutive man dressed in a security guard's uniform, although he was not here to protect the contents of the museum. Instead, he carried a sleek black satchel, a protective arm holding it tight to ensure it would not stray from his shoulder.

Hours earlier, when he entered the museum, this hall was filled with throngs of tourists milling around the exhibits and talking in hushed whispers. They followed the docents, and listened to self-guided audio tours, all the while dragging their bored children through room after dusty room. It had been easy to slip into a storage closet, scoped out days earlier, and wait until the hubbub died down and the museum closed for the day. He didn't even need to worry about the daily exit count ensuring that all the visitors who entered had left the building, because he gained entry through a back door when the catering service made their weekly delivery to the restaurant on the first floor. It was amazing how easy it was to snatch a silver tray loaded with croissants from the rear of the truck and stroll past the service door as if he belonged there. Discarding the white food service coat to reveal the guard uniform, he walked through the delivery dock and right into the museum. No one challenged him, and soon he was in place.

But now he must be careful not to leave any trace of his presence for the authorities to find later. The State Security Investigations Service, recently renamed to the gentler moniker of Homeland Security, was ruthless in their investigations and subsequent interrogations. He had no wish to become their unwilling guest.

He moved with an easy stealth, careful of his route, avoiding the path walked by the real guards and the coverage of the security cameras.

When he arrived at the far end of the empty hall, he ducked behind a pillar, and then made his way up a set of stone steps to the second level.

Skirting the balcony, the intruder passed by chambers containing mummified animals, canopic jars, ancient jewelry, and the prize of the museum, the golden death mask of King Tutankhamen.

But he was not here for any of this.

He ignored the displays of gold and jewels and kept walking until he arrived at a small chamber toward the far end of the balcony, within which was a raised stone dais, intricately carved on all four sides with hieroglyphics. Upon this lay an open sarcophagus enclosed in a glass case, and inside, the crumbling remains of a body, embalmed over three thousand years before and covered in tight cloth wrappings now yellowed and brittle with age.

The intruder stopped for a moment and observed the mummy, his head bowed in respect. Then, quickly, he slipped the leather satchel from his shoulder and lowered it to the floor, where it came to rest against the dais.

He kneeled and opened the bag, peering inside to make sure the contents were in order, and once satisfied, buckled the flap once more and stood. Without a backward glance, he turned, leaving the satchel against the exhibit, and hurried back through the museum. He retraced his steps, descending to the ground floor, and moved toward the main doors. But then he turned to the right, weaving his way through the first gallery until he reached an emergency exit door, which he pushed open.

Within moments he was outside, the cool night air a

welcome change from the oppressive afternoon heat that had lingered over the city when he entered the museum. He peeled off the uniform jacket and discarded it in a nearby trashcan, then loosened his shirt collar even as the alarms activated by the opened emergency exit alerted the guards inside that something was amiss.

Digging his hands deep into his pockets, the intruder strolled onto the concourse in front of the museum. He moved in the direction of the river, ignoring the few groups of tourists that lingered, taking in the sights of the ancient city.

As he reached the road and stepped onto the sidewalk, the boom of an explosion reached his ears.

He glanced around, slowing to watch the ball of orange fire and black acrid smoke that belched from the side of the museum. Then he turned away and kept on walking even as the screams of startled tourists filled the air and a faint wail of sirens drifted upon the breeze. It had begun.

TWO

NEW YORK CITY

THE MANSION on the Upper East Side was situated among lavish, meticulously groomed grounds so abundant that you would never know they were in the heart of one of the largest cities in the world, except for the faint rumble of cars and trucks that permeated the air.

Daniel Montague stood in a bay window at the front of the mansion and gazed out over the lush green landscape, a distant look in his eyes. Behind him, on an ornate coffee table fashioned from centuries old English Oak, sat the New York Times, opened to the international section. The headline across the top of the page, Bomb Destroys Priceless Artifacts at Cairo Museum, stood out in bold, black lettering.

He turned and crossed the room, his eyes straying to the newspaper as he passed by, and he felt a tug of fear because he knew who had set the device, and why.

Daniel entered a wide corridor with a window at one end. Sunlight arched through the glass, casting a checkerboard pattern across fine Asian rugs arranged atop polished wood floors with varnish the color of cherries. The light splashed up the wall, straining to reach the first in a series of papyrus that sat behind museum glass frames. Each one was thousands of years old. The most ancient, badly fragmented and almost unrecognizable, harkened back to the Old Kingdom's Fifth Dynasty, some forty-four centuries before. These objects were priceless and would not be out of place in the British Museum or the Smithsonian. Instead, they rested in a private collection that would be the envy of most curators. Deeper in the house were other objects of equal importance collected over a lifetime; some had been purchased, others were unearthed on his own expeditions.

He reached the end of the corridor, coming to a locked door, and drew a key from his pocket. This was his study, and it contained some of the most prized pieces in the collection. He went to his desk, ignoring the shelves lined with ancient jars, amulets, and clay statues, and sat down.

He removed a legal pad from the desk drawer and started to write, the words scrawled and hasty. Then he folded the sheet and slipped it into an envelope before taking up the pen once more and addressing it in the same fast hand.

That done, Daniel stood and retreated from the room, moving quickly through the house until he reached a set of wide double doors, each with six intricately engraved panels. These he opened and stepped outside.

Hurrying through the gardens, Daniel followed the driveway to the wrought-iron gates and opened the mailbox. He slipped the letter inside and turned to walk away. As he did so, his eyes wandered to the road and the black SUV crawling toward the estate. He paused, watching, as it came to a halt at the curb with the engine idling.

Daniel caught his breath. Ordinarily the sight of a car stopped on the street would go unnoticed. But not today. There was something sinister about the way the car lingered opposite the gates, its tinted windows blocking any view of the occupants.

Forcing his gaze away, Daniel turned and hurried back to the house. Time was short, and there was still one thing he must do.

Entering the lobby, he closed the double doors and drew hefty bolts across before turning to the security system keypad and entering the code. When the box beeped twice to let him know the system was active, he breathed a little easier.

Making his way back through the house, Daniel returned to the study. Moments later, his task complete, he went to the living room, to the bay window overlooking the grounds.

His eyes scanned the landscape.

He could not see the gates from his vantage point, but he was sure the black SUV was still there, watching. Waiting.

Daniel lingered at the window. They would be coming soon, he was sure. The explosion and subsequent fire that destroyed several galleries at the Cairo Museum was a world away from the Upper East Side, but he had known what it meant the second his eyes fell upon that headline. The timing was too exact to be coincidence.

At least they would not find what they wanted. If he hurried, they would not find him either. He owned several properties, a few of which were known only to his closest confidants, and if he could reach one of those, he would be safe.

He turned and hurried back to the study. When he arrived

there, he opened his desk drawer and retrieved the keys for his Mercedes parked in the four-car garage at the rear.

It was at that moment that the power went off.

Daniel froze.

Why hadn't he put his cell phone in his pocket instead of leaving it charging on the nightstand next to the bed? It was a stupid mistake.

There was a landline on his desk. A holdover he kept for emergencies.

He reached out and scooped up the receiver.

Silence.

The phone line was dead. He was alone.

Daniel took a step toward the door, car keys in hand. He must get out of the house right now and make his escape.

But it was already too late.

A faint noise reached his ears from the corridor outside his study. It was nothing more than the creak of a floorboard, but unusual enough to give Daniel pause.

He stifled a gasp of fear, his eyes fixed on the door. His hands trembled. When he saw the two black-clad figures appear, masks disguising their faces, his throat tightened.

"I was wondering when you would show up." Daniel spoke the words in a voice as steady as he could muster.

"Where is it, old man?" the closer of the two figures entered the room.

"Somewhere you will never find it." Daniel resisted the urge to run. It would do him no good.

"Don't play games with me. Hand it over."

"I don't think so."

"Don't be stupid," the intruder said. "Don't make us do things the hard way."

"It doesn't matter." Daniel felt his voice crack. "Either way, I'm dead."

"True, but you can make your journey into the afterlife less painful if you cooperate."

The men were close now. Daniel retreated backwards toward the window until his legs contacted the sill. He wondered if he could turn and crash through the glass, escape onto the grounds. But it was pointless, he knew. There would be others outside, waiting for him to run. They had covered all the eventualities, he was sure.

"You don't scare me," Daniel lied.

"So be it." The man shrugged. "You have the right to choose your own path."

"I won't talk." Daniel felt his legs buckling. "You will leave here empty-handed."

"We'll see about that." The intruder circled Daniel, never taking his eyes off the older man. He turned and signaled to his partner. "Why don't we get started?"

THREE

NYPD HOMICIDE DETECTIVE John Decker was not in a good mood. Looking at the bloody, torn up remains of what used to be a living, breathing person was a hell of a way to start the day.

He was still in bed when the call came in, much too early. He had staggered to the bathroom, noting the disheveled brown hair, the bags under his eyes, which looked almost gray in the dim light but were normally a bright blue. Most of the time he thought his mid-thirties had been kind, barely aging his face, but today he looked like crap. He wished he'd gone to bed earlier, gotten a good night's rest. He splashed a handful of water on his face, blinking to clear the sleep from his eyes, and was on his way in less than ten minutes.

Now he stood still, a cup of tepid coffee in his hand, and allowed the gruesome sight to come into focus. The victim, strapped to his own office chair, looked like he had been beaten for hours. His linen shirt, originally white, was now stained a deep crimson, matching the streaks that lined his face like a road map. Deep, angry bruises, yellow and purple, covered what little skin was not crusted with dried blood, and one eye bulged from its socket, the flesh around it angry and swollen. The man's hands had been duct taped to the chair's armrests. His fingers had been snapped backwards and now rested at unnatural angles.

Decker grimaced and tried to push the thought of what must have occurred from his mind, opting instead to focus his energy on the surroundings.

The mansion, sitting in one of New York's most affluent neighborhoods, was not your typical crime scene. Usually it was a back alley, a crack house in Harlem, or a floater in the Hudson River. Murder was a squalid act, and the current genteel surroundings only highlighted the brutal nature of the act he was here to investigate.

"Once in a while it would be nice if people got themselves murdered at a reasonable hour." Ryan Connor, Decker's partner, leaned on the doorframe, his casual manner at odds with the reason they were there.

"You got somewhere better to be?" Decker asked.

"Na. Still, I'm glad I had breakfast before I came out here," Connor said, his mouth a thin line. "Not that it's sitting very well right now. Jesus. This is the worst part of this job."

"Yeah." Decker glanced down at his coffee. The brown liquid was a welcome break from looking at the murder victim. Behind him, in the hallway, a dumpy middle-aged woman sat on a chair, dabbing a white handkerchief to her tear-streaked face. "What did she say?"

"The usual," Connor replied. "She's the cleaner. Arrived at around six to start her shift and found the body. She made the 911 call."

"That's a little early to be dusting, isn't it?"

"Exactly what I said." Connor ran a hand through his black, wiry hair. "But apparently that's how our victim liked it. He was an early riser by all accounts."

"This crime scene doesn't make sense." Decker took a sip of the coffee, then scowled, resisting the urge to toss the cup.

"I'm not sure I follow." Connor shook his head. "Seems pretty straightforward to me. There are signs of forced entry, the security system has been disabled, and the power was cut at the meter box. I'm figuring home invasion robbery gone wrong."

"Maybe." Decker looked around, his eyes alighting on the vast collection of valuable artifacts in the room. "But why go to all that trouble and leave this stuff behind? It must be worth a fortune."

"Have you got a better theory?"

"This man wasn't just killed, he was tortured." Decker did his best to keep his gaze averted from the corpse. "There's more to this than simple robbery. They beat him, cut him. They even broke his fingers one by one. Whoever did this wanted something, and they wanted it bad."

"Question is, did they get it?" Connor replied.

"Hard to say since we don't know what they were looking for," Decker said. "But my guess would be no."

"Huh?"

"This man died during torture. That doesn't make sense if the perpetrators got what they came for. Anyone willing to commit this kind of atrocity would have no compunction killing in cold blood, and they would certainly not want a witness. Neither would they take the time to continue torturing the victim once they had their answers. If they got what they wanted, this man would have a gunshot wound."

"See, now that's why I like being your partner. You make us both look good." Connor grinned.

"Yeah," Decker said. "But none of this tells us what they came here for. Was it an object, or did they want information?"

"Good question," Connor replied. "Whatever it was, they sure went to a lot of trouble. This thing was well planned and executed."

"They must have been casing the place for days, figuring out how to get in, following the victim." Decker looked thoughtful. "Maybe they showed up on a camera somewhere."

"Yeah, I thought of that. The mansion has surveillance on the first floor, but it was taken down when the electric was cut. Smart bastards even disabled the backup generator which normally would have powered the security system in the event of a power issue," Connor said. "There are cameras outside too, around the perimeter of the grounds, so we may get a hit from one of those, but I wouldn't hold your breath. These guys were pros."

"What about the street?"

"Nothing. Closest camera is on a traffic light two blocks away," Connor said. "Even if it did record the perpetrators, it will be impossible to know which vehicle is theirs. That intersection gets fifty cars a minute."

Decker blinked as a flash went off, the crime scene photographer snapping yet another photo. "There's not much more we can do here. Might as well let forensics finish up." He moved into the hallway. "Maybe if we're lucky, they'll pull a nice, easy set of prints or two, and we'll be busting a perp by day's end."

"Ever the optimist," Connor said.

"A guy can dream." Decker looked down at his coffee cup. "Come on, I need to get a decent cup of coffee."

FOUR

AT FOUR O'CLOCK THAT AFTERNOON, Emma Wilson sat in her office overlooking Central Park and gazed out of the window. She never grew tired of the view, the sprawling green oasis surrounded by a concrete forest of skyscrapers. From her vantage point three floors high, she could see the cars and trucks moving along Central Park West, and beyond that, a line of trees marking the edge of the park itself. A small smudge of nature resisting the encroachment of mankind.

When the office door opened, she swiveled to find Herb Johnson, curator-in-charge of ancient antiquities, standing there in his tweed jacket. A slightly askew red bow tie did nothing to shake the image of stuffy academia.

"You're back." He lingered in the doorway. "How was Egypt?"

"Hot," Emma replied. She picked up an object from her desk, an Ushabti no larger than her palm. She turned the small, carved funerary statue over and studied it for a moment before speaking again. "Three months of digging and I'm still no closer to finding Ramesses than before."

"You gave it a good shot," Herb said. "The research was solid. More than solid. It was good enough to get the museum to fund the dig, which is no small feat."

"I still failed." Emma laid the statue back on the desk. "I wasted the department's money, not to mention dragging a whole team of people and truckloads of equipment out into the desert on a fool's errand. I really thought I knew where the tomb was."

"Don't be too hard on yourself." Herb smiled. "Howard Carter spent years looking for Tut. The Valley of the Kings does not give up its secrets easily. One short expedition is nothing. Do more research, then go back next year and try again."

"Next year," echoed Emma. "We were lucky to get permits this time around. Who knows if there will be another chance?"

"Well, if there isn't, you have plenty to occupy you right here." Herb nodded in the general direction of the exhibit halls. "Besides, you found some good artifacts."

"Which are still stuck in Cairo because the Egyptian government won't allow them out of the country, so I can't even study the few pieces I did find."

"Red tape. They will release them eventually." He paused. "Of course, it could take years, given the present political climate, and if they deem them important cultural artifacts…"

"If you're trying to cheer me up, you're not doing a very good job." Emma leaned back in her chair.

"I know. Anyway, I'm glad you're back. The place wasn't the same without you."

"Thanks." Emma forced a smile.

"Tell you what, I have a meeting right now, but why don't

you swing by my office after work. We'll hit the town. I'll buy you a drink or two, take the edge off."

"Can I get a rain check on that?" Emma asked. "I would really like to go home and get an early night. I'm not sure my body has realized I'm in a different time zone yet."

"If you change your mind, you know where I am." Herb turned to leave, then backtracked. He reached into his jacket pocket and brought out a flat white envelope. "I almost forgot. This came for you today."

"For me?"

"That's what it says." Herb held the letter out.

"Thanks." Emma took the envelope and stared at it for a long minute. There was no clue regarding the sender, only her name and the museum address written in spidery cursive. "How mysterious."

"Quite." Herb was almost out of the office now. "Let me know if you change your mind on that drink."

"I will." Emma watched him go and then turned her attention back to the envelope. She hardly ever got mail at the museum, and when she did, it was usually official business, dig permits or some other mundane paperwork.

This was different.

She ran a finger along the edge of the envelope, pausing at the corner, her nail sliding under the sealed flap. She hesitated, overwhelmed by a sudden sense of dread, but then, shaking off the strange feeling, she ripped the envelope and slipped two fingers inside to remove the folded sheet of paper within.

She looked at the letter, penned in the same untidy hand as the envelope. Her eyes fell to the bottom of the sheet, to the sender's signature, solving the mystery of the sender.

But why would he write a letter to her? It would be so much easier to pick up the phone or send an email.

With a returning sense of misgiving, she began to read.

When she was done, Emma read the letter again, slower this time, and then picked up her cell phone and made a call.

The phone rang.

She waited, her fingers drumming on the desk.

The call clicked over to voicemail. The familiar baritone voice of a man she hadn't spoken to in three years filled her ears, his clipped Ivy League accent the same as she remembered.

She hung up and thought for a moment, then rose, grabbed her jacket off the back of the chair, and hurried from the room, pushing the letter into her pocket as she did so.

FIVE

JOHN DECKER LEANED back in his chair and closed his eyes, the haunting image of the dead Daniel Montague immediately coming into focus. He did his best to push the memories away. He'd investigated many murders and seen some awful things, but the sheer brutality of the wounds inflicted upon the millionaire shocked him. Even so, he ran through the crime scene once more in his mind's eye, looking for any small detail that he might have missed.

Something struck his face, stinging.

He opened his eyes to find a paperclip sitting on the desk in front of him. He looked at his partner. "Was that you?"

"Had to get your attention somehow," Connor said, playing with a second paper clip. "You zoning out on me there, buddy?"

"I was thinking," Decker replied, annoyed. "Going over the scene in my mind. Looking for clues."

"Yeah, well, you won't find any of those inside your head,"

Connor replied. He pointed in the vague direction of the exit. "Out there, man. That's where the answers are, and our killer."

"Except that we don't have any idea where to start looking."

"Yeah." Connor nodded. He twisted the paper clip until it broke, then dropped it in the trash and plucked another one from a small plastic container on his desk. "I was thinking about that. Whoever did this was clever. They left no prints, no DNA. Hell, we don't even know how many of them there were."

"Ghosts." Decker sat up and flipped through the coroner's report, lingering on the pages detailing the torture inflicted upon the victim. "A professional hit squad."

"Maybe we should hit the streets, see if any of the usual suspects know anything."

"It's better than sitting here and staring at the walls, I guess." Decker closed the folder and stood, grabbing his coat. "You got any idea where to start?"

"I was thinking we go down to Murphy's." Connor slipped on a black leather jacket, zipped it up. "If anyone knows anything, it'll be one of the lowlifes hanging out there."

"Makes sense." Decker nodded.

Murphy's Pub was a dive in Hell's Kitchen. It was a holdout from the days when the area was a rough immigrant neighborhood, and it somehow still kept going despite rising rents. It was also a favorite watering hole for many of Manhattan's more savory denizens.

He rounded the desk, was about to join Connor, when he saw two figures approaching. One was the desk sergeant. The other was an attractive, petite woman in her early thirties, with long brown hair and a trim figure. He had never seen her before, and he wondered who she was.

He was about to find out.

"Decker." The desk sergeant spoke in his broad New York accent. "This here is Miss Emma Wilson. I think you might want to talk to her about the Montague case."

"Really?" Decker exchanged a look with his partner.

"Hello," the woman said as she drew close. "Pleased to make your acquaintance." She held her hand out.

"Likewise." Decker shook her hand. "How can we help you, Miss Wilson?"

"Emma, please." Her eyes met his for a moment, and Decker was taken aback by their shimmering blue intensity. "And it's more what I can do for you."

"I see." Decker gestured toward the desk. "Take a seat."

The desk sergeant watched Emma pull up a chair and then turned away, retreating back in the direction of the station's lobby.

"You're in charge of the murder investigation into Daniel Montague's death?" Emma asked.

"I am," Decker replied, settling back into his own seat. "Along with my partner here, Ryan Connor."

"Good." She paused and bit her lip, then spoke again. "Daniel was a good friend of mine. I went to his home this afternoon to speak with him and found a police officer stationed at the gates. He told me what happened and gave me your name."

"I see," Decker said. "Why do you think you can help us?"

"I used to work with Daniel, although I hadn't seen him for years. We traveled to Egypt together several times. I'm sure you saw all the antiquities in his home."

"We did." Decker wondered what all this was leading up to. "Quite a collection."

"He found many of those pieces himself. He was a very smart man, had a fascination with ancient Egypt. I think he thought of himself as a modern-day Lord Carnarvon to my Howard Carter." Emma paused and wiped a tear from her cheek. "A grand financier."

"With regard to what?"

"Expeditions," Emma said. "I'm an Egyptologist working out of the Museum of Natural History. Daniel funded several of my digs. He participated in all of them himself. It was a stipulation of the funding. He wasn't formally trained. He made his money in real estate, but he was an excellent amateur archeologist even so."

"You hadn't seen him for several years?"

"No. We didn't see eye to eye on a few things and went our separate ways. I thought about patching things up, but never made the effort. Now it's too late."

"So how can you help our investigation if you haven't spoken with him recently?"

"Because of this." Emma reached into her pocket and pulled out a creased envelope, laying it on the desk. She slipped two fingers inside and drew out a folded sheet of notepaper. "He wrote to me. I got the letter this afternoon. It was rambling, strange. I thought he might be going mad, but then I went to his house and…" Her voice trailed off.

"Take your time. It's okay." Decker leaned close, touched her arm, a small gesture of reassurance.

"I'm sorry. I'm in shock. I can't believe he's gone." Emma took a deep breath.

"May I?" Decker lifted the letter.

"Sure."

"Thank you." He took the scrap of paper, unfolded it, and started to read aloud.

Emma

I know we haven't talked for a very long time, and I am truly sorry for that, but now I feel I must reach out to you. Have you heard the news about the Cairo Museum? You know what that means. The Brotherhood is real. I have hidden the object somewhere they will not find it, in a safe place. If anything happens to me, if they kill me, you must make sure it never falls into their hands. If nothing else, you must do that, or the consequences will be catastrophic.

I am sorry to put this burden upon you. Please know that if there were any other way, I would not do so.

Always remember Thebes.

Your friend forever,

Daniel

Decker folded the letter and put it back in its envelope. He opened his drawer and took out a clear plastic bag and dropped the note inside. "I have to keep this for evidence, at least for now."

"I know. I guessed as much," Emma replied.

Connor leaned forward. "What object is he referring to, Emma?"

"There's only one object that comes to mind. It's the reason we haven't talked in years."

"And?" Decker prodded her.

"A statue of Anubis I discovered on our final dig near the ancient city of Thebes on the western bank of the Nile." She trailed off, a distant look coming upon her, as if she were remembering something painful. "It was perfect, magnificent. One of the finest examples ever found. It's made of ebony, with solid silver claws, gold leaf and obsidian accents. It should have gone to the Egyptian authorities, the Supreme Council of Antiquities, for cataloguing, but Daniel was afraid they would not release it back to us, so he smuggled it out of the country behind my back. I was livid. I'm a researcher, not a tomb robber. I wanted to bring it back through the proper channels. That was the last time we spoke."

"And you think the statue has something to with what happened to him?"

"Maybe."

"What's this Brotherhood he mentions, and what does it have to do with the Cairo Museum?"

"The Brotherhood of Anubis. They were a powerful cult in ancient Egypt. Rumors have persisted that they are still around, waiting for the right time to resurrect their god, who will judge the entire human race one by one, sparing only the worthy. There are only a few brief moments over the millennia that match the conditions needed for the resurrection, according to the legend."

"And now is one of those moments?" Decker asked.

"Yes. It has to do with the path of Comet Artemus I."

"Never heard of it," Connor said.

"Few people have. It's a relatively little-known comet, but it comes around once every thousand years, and more important, it's visible from the African continent. The Egyptians were master astronomers and would have known about the comet, even if they didn't know what it was. It's not surprising that a resurrection myth sprung up around it."

"And the comet is due for a return?"

"It will be at its closest point to Earth in over a thousand years during the next few days."

"That still doesn't explain how the museum in Cairo fits in."

"Because the only way to resurrect the God Anubis is to

destroy his earthly remains or, more precisely, the remains of the pharaoh they believe to be his mortal host. His spirit will then take harbor in a graven image of the god while it waits to be transferred to a new, living body."

"A graven image?"

"Yes. The god's spirit is supposed to inhabit the statue we found on our last dig. The one Daniel stole. There were hiero-glyphic writings in the tomb we were excavating, outlining the resurrection process. It was most precise."

"And you think this Brotherhood of Anubis destroyed the mummy in the museum and then came after the statue?" Decker asked.

"Daniel certainly did, at least if the letter is any indication."

"And you?"

"I think it's ridiculous. Nothing more than half-baked theo-ries spread by badly researched pseudo documentaries and conspiracy theorists."

"Even so, someone killed him, tortured him, for something," Decker said. "And it clearly wasn't his vast collection of antiqui-ties, which must be worth a fortune. They are still there. Besides, if they broke in to steal the collection, why bother to torture him?"

"Because they were after one object in particular," Connor speculated.

"The statue," Decker said.

Connor nodded. "The question is, did they get it?"

"Daniel said he hid it." Emma nodded toward the letter. "And he even told me where."

"I don't follow," Decker said. "There's nothing in the letter to indicate that."

"But there is," Emma countered. "He said he put the statue

in a safe place. I think he meant his floor safe. I'm one of the few people he told about it, and it would be almost impossible to find if you didn't know where to look."

"Then what are we waiting for?" Decker said, excited. Finally, they had a break. "We need to look in that safe."

SIX

DECKER AND CONNOR led Emma past the police sentry guarding the main entrance of the mansion on the Upper East Side and into the house.

As soon as they were inside, Decker turned to Emma. "Where's the safe?"

"This way." Emma took off at a clip through the lobby toward the rear of the building. "It's under the floor in the study."

"The study?" Decker raised an eyebrow, shooting a sideways glance toward his partner. "That's where the body was found."

"Oh." Emma faltered for a moment. "Is it out of bounds or something, being the murder scene and all?"

"We'll be fine. Forensics have already gone over the place." Decker followed Emma to the study door, which was still draped with yellow crime scene tape. "But don't touch anything unless you have to."

"Got it." Emma ducked under the tape and then waited for the two policemen to join her.

She turned and examined the room, stiffening when she saw the chair, pieces of duct tape still attached, a crimson stain dried on the floor beneath.

"Are you okay?" Decker asked.

"Sure." Emma took a deep breath. "It's unnerving, seeing everything like this."

"I know," Decker replied, sensing her unease. "If you are not up to it, you can tell us where the safe is and wait outside."

"No." Emma forced a smile. "I'll be okay. It's just seeing where he died, the blood, that chair, it all feels so real all of a sudden."

"Take your time, Miss Wilson," Connor said. "There's no rush."

"The safe is over here." Emma moved into the room, giving the chair, and the bloodstain, a wide berth. She went behind the desk, then dropped to the floor, disappearing from view.

Decker joined her, careful not to disturb anything. "He put the safe down here?"

"Yes." Emma pulled back an ornate rug and felt around on the floor, her fingers tracing the line of the floorboards.

"I don't see anything."

"Wait. You will." Emma found what she was searching for. She placed her finger into a depression in the floorboard, almost imperceptible if you didn't know it was there. She pressed down and exerted pressure sideways. There was a click followed by a whir of tiny motors, and a piece of the floor moved back, sliding away to reveal a flat steel door tucked into a recess underneath. The door had a square keypad. "I told you it would be impossible to find if you didn't know it was here."

"A false panel." Decker had to admit, he was impressed by the millionaire's craftiness. He eyed the keypad. "I don't suppose you know the safe code."

"Nope."

Decker's heart fell. "So why did he send you the letter?"

"Because he knew I would figure it out." Emma reached down and tapped the keypad, her fingers picking out six digits. The light above the pad flashed red. "Dammit."

"What number was that?"

"The date we found the statue. 091608. September 16, 2008. I was sure that must be it."

"Are there any other numbers that would mean anything to both of you?" Decker was frustrated.

"Not that I can think of." Emma sighed. "I have no idea when his birthday was, or his social security number, not that he would use either of those - too obvious. I'm at a loss."

"Maybe there was a clue in the letter."

"I don't know." Emma's brows furrowed, as if she were deep in thought.

"It would be something only you would understand."

"Because if the letter got intercepted, he wouldn't want the thieves to know the safe combination."

"Exactly."

"I still don't..." Emma paused, her eyes widening. "Wait. I have an idea."

"What?"

"*Always remember Thebes.* That's how he signed off. An odd thing to say in a letter like that, don't you think?" Emma tapped the keypad again. There was a moment of silence, then a clunk as the bolts disengaged. The light on the keypad flashed green.

"It worked." Decker kneeled down next to her. "Good job."

"But how?" Connor hovered near the desk. "There were no numbers in the letter."

"Thebes. The location where we found the statue." Emma was speaking fast now, excited. "He really was a clever man."

"You still haven't explained," said Decker.

"Daniel knew I would remember the coordinates of the dig, the exact location we found the statue. 25°43′14″N 32°36′17″E. The safe needs a six-digit code. All I did was add each of the six numbers together to come up with the correct sequence of buttons to push. 7-7-5-5-9-8. Simple."

"For you, maybe." Connor said.

"Montague wasn't the only smart one," Decker agreed. "What are you waiting for? Open it up."

"Here goes." Emma gripped the handle and lifted the door, swinging it upward to reveal an oblong metal box. Inside, swathed in shadows, was an object eighteen inches long wrapped in a slip of cloth.

"Is that it?" Decker peered closely, trying to get a better look.

"This is the statue, I'm sure." Emma reached in and gripped the object, lifting it gently from its resting place. She stood and moved to the desk, laying it on the surface, and then lifted the cloth to reveal a stunning sight.

The statue was in perfect condition. The deep black ebony looked like it could have been carved yesterday. The silver claws and gold accents glinted in the weak light filtering through the window.

Decker repressed a shudder as he gazed upon the jackal-headed figure, so realistic he almost believed it could rear up at any moment.

Emma reached out and ran a hand across the length of the

statue, her touch light and respectful. She looked up at the two detectives, her eyes sparkling. "Gentlemen, I'd like you to meet Anubis, Egyptian Lord of the underworld."

SEVEN

"WHAT HAPPENS NOW?" Emma asked. "It seems a shame for such a fantastic piece of history to end up in the bowels of a police station."

It was late in the evening and they were back on the second floor at the precinct house, huddled around Decker's desk, with the statue laid out in front of them.

"It won't be forever," Decker said. "Once the investigation is over, we'll release it."

"But to who?" Emma looked distressed.

"That's a good question. Usually it would go back to the family of the deceased, but there are extenuating circumstances in this case." Decker scratched his head. "It was illegally smuggled out of Egypt, after all. The Egyptian authorities might want a say in the statue's fate."

"I know."

"And you said yourself that Daniel Montague should have gone through the proper channels. It was this very object that caused the argument between the two of you."

"It should be returned to Cairo, but still…" Her eyes drifted along the sleek form, a wistful look coming upon her.

"It does have a certain allure." Connor leaned in close. "The eyes are almost hypnotic."

"In a gruesome kind of way." Decker shuddered. The statue gave him the creeps. "The sooner we get this thing locked up and safe, the better, if you ask me."

"I agree." Emma turned away. "Every time I cross paths with this statue something bad happens. First it drove a wedge between me and Daniel. Now it's cost him his life. Maybe it should go back to Egypt."

"Not until it goes to the evidence locker," Connor said. He glanced at Decker. "I'll do the honors if you like?"

"Sure." Decker lifted the cloth and laid it back over the statue. He watched Connor pick the statue up, cradling it in his arms before placing it inside a white cardboard evidence box and securing the lid.

"Take care with it," Emma said, turning to Connor. "It's very old."

"I'll be careful." Connor lifted the box and moved off in the direction of the elevators, before glancing back toward Decker. "I'm beat. My shift should have ended two hours ago. I'm going to take off after I drop this in evidence."

"Sure thing." Decker nodded. "I'm not far behind."

"I should go home too," Emma said, her eyes trailing Connor and the statue as he disappeared into the elevator. "It's been a hell of a day, and I only got back from the Middle East yesterday. I'm looking forward to a good night's sleep."

"Okay."

"Unless you still need to ask more questions?" Emma asked.

"No. I think we're all done here. You've been most helpful, Miss Wilson." Decker smiled. "But if you think of anything else that might be pertinent, let me know."

"I will," Emma replied. She turned to leave, then hesitated, her brow furrowed. "Do you think he suffered?"

"The truth?" Decker narrowed his eyes.

"Yes."

"What they did to him was not nice."

"I see." A cloud passed over her face, and Decker wondered if it was fear or regret. "Thank you for being so frank with me."

"Will you be alright?" Decker asked. "I could have a patrol car swing by and check on you later this evening."

"I'm a big girl. Besides, I'll be going straight to bed. But I appreciate the gesture."

"Here, take this." Decker picked up a business card emblazoned with the NYPD logo. He flipped it over and grabbed a pen, wrote a number on the reverse, then held it out to her. "This is my personal phone. If you need anything, call me. Any time of day or night."

"Thank you." She took the card and tucked it into her pocket. "That makes me feel much better." She lingered a moment longer, her eyes catching Decker's for a brief second, but then she looked away before moving off toward the elevators.

Decker watched her leave, and then sat back down at his desk, his mind replaying the day's events. Something felt off. A sense of unease hovered over him. A vague feeling that lingered even though he could not think of any reason to feel that way.

He opened his laptop, brought the web browser up, and typed three words into the search bar.

Brotherhood of Anubis.

The browser returned several pages of results. He skimmed them, ignoring those that were not relevant, and was left with a paltry two matches.

He clicked on the first. The website was amateur to say the least, with yellow text on a bright blue background. It hurt his eyes to read the page, and when he did, he came to the conclusion that there was nothing useful there. It was all crazy rantings that lacked any real cohesion, the stuff of an addled mind. The one paragraph that did mention the Brotherhood of Anubis blamed them for everything from the fall of Rome to the disappearance of Amelia Earhart, and even claimed a link to the Roswell incident. Decker found it hard to believe that aliens crashed their spaceship while visiting Earth to connect with an ancient Egyptian cult, and so he hit the back button and moved on to the only other relevant hit.

This one was more promising, being the website of a large, well-respected university. However, upon examining the contents of the page, he discovered that the mention was nothing more than a brief reference in a wider text talking about ancient religions that existed prior to the rise of Christianity.

He closed the browser.

This was a waste of time.

If the Brotherhood of Anubis was still around and tied to the death of Daniel Montague, he wasn't going to make the connection by browsing the web.

He leaned back in his chair and closed his eyes. It had been a long day, and he was tired. There was nothing more he could do tonight, and things would be clearer in the morning, he was sure. He stood and grabbed his jacket, pulling it on as he made his way to the elevators.

As he stood waiting, Decker's thoughts lingered on the statue, and the cult Emma believed were hunting for it. A sudden chill overtook him, and he shuddered. Was there really a Brotherhood of Anubis out there, on the streets of New York, hell bent on resurrecting an ancient god? It sounded implausible... Except that someone had tortured Daniel Montague and murdered him. That much was a given. Ancient cult or not, there were sadistic killers on the loose. Decker only hoped he could find them before someone else died.

EIGHT

AT TEN-THIRTY THAT NIGHT, Emma Wilson moved through her apartment located in the swanky neighborhood of Brooklyn Heights across the East River from Manhattan. The residence, occupying the ground floor of a brownstone dating to the early eighteen-hundreds, was much more than she could ever have afforded on her museum salary, but she didn't have to. Three years earlier, a distant aunt had passed away and left her the home, and all of its contents. Though the décor was more contemporary than Emma's classical taste, she'd been focused on her work at the museum and hadn't yet taken the time to put her personal touch on the apartment.

She went into the bedroom and undressed, her mind stuck on the horrific events of the day. A lump formed in her throat when she thought of Daniel. Seeing that chair in his study, with the tape still attached where he was tied, made her stomach churn. She wished she had gotten one last chance to talk to him and patch things up. But that would never happen now.

Slipping into a thin cotton nightgown, she crawled into bed and closed her eyes, relishing the feel of the cool silken sheets on her body. It wasn't long before she was drifting off, floating into a deep and dreamless sleep. Until a sound somewhere beyond the bedroom pulled her back. Emma knew every creak and moan of the old apartment, and this was out of place. Jarring. Then, as quickly as it had arrived, the sound was gone.

Emma opened her eyes and held her breath, listening. She strained to hear the sound again, but all she heard was the rustling of leaves as the breeze wafted through the bushes outside her bedroom window and the distant rumble of cars moving through the dark streets.

She stayed like that for several seconds until her unease faded. It was probably nothing, a cat creeping along the windowsill outside, or a neighbor moving around in the apartment upstairs.

She turned over, pushing her hand under the pillow, and closed her eyes again.

No sooner had she done so than the sound came again - a low shuffle, like stealthy feet - on the wood floors in her hallway.

She sat upright, her heart pounding.

This was no neighbor clanking around in another part of the building. This was in her apartment, she was sure.

Emma reached across the nightstand and clicked on the lamp, relieved to see that her bedroom was empty. Even so, she hunted for her phone.

It was nowhere to be found.

With a deepening sense of dread, she realized the phone was still in her coat pocket, along with the business card given to her by the detective, John Decker. And the coat was hanging on a hook next to the front door. If someone was in the apartment, they would be blocking her only means to call for help.

She cursed her own stupidity.

Why hadn't she kept the phone close? What was she thinking? Now she wished she had taken the detective up on his offer of sending a car by to check up on her. The sight of a police cruiser might have dissuaded anyone intent upon breaking into the apartment.

It didn't matter now. There was no point dwelling on what she should have done. Emma pulled back the sheets and slipped out of bed, ignoring the chill as her bare feet made contact with the wood floor.

She tiptoed to the bedroom door and opened it a crack, peering through the narrow gap, but could see nothing amiss.

Taking a deep breath, she inched the door open a little wider, her eyes roaming the dark hallway beyond.

Could she have imagined the noises?

She had been on edge ever since that afternoon, her mind returning again and again to Daniel and the way he died. It was no wonder her mind would turn every little sound into something ominous. On a normal day she wouldn't even think twice about such things, but today was not a normal day.

She stepped out into the hall, glancing both ways to make sure no one was lurking there. Apart from the bedroom, there were two more doors leading off the hallway. One was the bathroom and other was the living room. Both doors were closed, just as she had left them. Further along, an archway led into the kitchen, which she could see was empty.

That left two places to check.

The living room was closer, so she would take care of that room first. She pushed the door open.

It creaked inward, revealing the dark space beyond, lit only by the dim light from a streetlamp on the sidewalk outside. Long shadows stretched across the floor like creeping, skeletal fingers. She suppressed a shudder and steeled herself to step across the threshold.

At that moment, she felt a sharp, forceful blow from behind.

She cried out and toppled forward, hitting the floor so hard the wind was knocked from her. She gasped and rolled over, scooting backward as a dark shape loomed. Behind her attacker was a second figure, also dressed in black. Both wore facemasks that obscured their features.

"Who are you?" she croaked, her breath coming in short, shallow gasps. "What do you want?"

In reply, the closest figure reached down, grabbed her arm in a vice-like grip. He pulled Emma to her feet and dragged her back into the bedroom.

Her mind reeled. Were these the same people who had killed Daniel? More to the point, were they going to kill *her*?

She dug her heels in, fought against her captors, but it did no good, and soon she was thrown down onto the bed.

"Do you have the statue?" The larger of the intruders spoke, his accent familiar.

Egyptian.

"What statue?" Her voice sounded small and hollow.

"The statue of Anubis. Give it to us."

"I don't have it."

"But you know where it is."

"No." She gritted her teeth. "Even if I did know, I wouldn't tell you. I know what you did to Daniel."

"All the more reason to tell us what we want to know." The

figure advanced. His partner circled around to the other side of the bed.

Emma had no idea what was going to happen next, but she knew it would hurt, and she had no intention of succumbing without a fight.

She reached out, her hand curling around the shaft of the lamp on her nightstand. In a swift movement, she lifted it and swung it at the larger of the two intruders.

The lamp was heavy, made of cast iron.

It caught her assailant a glancing blow across the temple.

The lampshade crumpled, the bulb shattered, and the room was plunged into darkness. A moment later the cord went taut as it reached its full length, and then the plug came free of the electrical outlet.

The intruder staggered backward with a cry of alarm.

Emma jumped up from the bed.

The other assailant sprinted forward.

She swung the lamp again, hitting the advancing intruder on the shoulder. The jolt ripped the makeshift weapon from her grip, and it clattered to the floor.

But it had bought her enough time to flee.

With both attackers reeling, Emma bolted for freedom.

She tore into the hallway and turned left.

The front door was mere steps away.

But it might as well have been a mile.

A hand gripped her nightgown. She was yanked roughly back toward the bedroom. The neckline rode up, choking her.

She twisted and struggled to break free, relieved to find that only one of the assailants had followed her into the hallway. The other one, whom she had hit in the face, was still on the ground, dazed.

He would not stay that way for long.

She either escaped now, or she would be dead.

She swung a fist toward the remaining attacker. The blow caught her assailant under the chin, but glanced off, harmless.

She brought her fist up to strike again, but this time her attacker was ready, pulling her forward so that there was no room to land the punch.

Emma struggled, frantic, her hands finding the assailant's facemask.

She tugged.

The mask came away and Emma found herself looking at a young woman with dark, tanned skin and short, cropped blonde hair.

For a moment Emma was taken aback, surprised that the intruder was female, but then she saw her chance. She reached up quickly and pressed her thumbs into the other woman's eyeballs, gouging them hard.

The intruder screeched in pain and let go, stumbling backwards, hands flying up to her eyes.

Emma didn't waste the opportunity.

She turned and fled, grabbing her coat as she pulled the front door open and ran out into the night. She hurried down the front steps onto the street beyond. It was only when she reached a main road several blocks away that she slowed, sobs wracking her body.

Slipping the coat over her nightgown, Emma found the card that Detective Decker had given to her. With shaking hands, she took out her phone and dialed the number on the back of the card.

While she waited for Decker to answer, her mind strayed to the strange female attacker, and something she had noticed when she pulled the mask off. There, on the woman's neck, was a small tattoo inked in black of a seated jackal in profile, surrounded by an oval with a horizontal line at one end.

A cartouche.

She shivered, a sudden fear overtaking her, because she recognized the ancient symbol, and she knew what it meant.

The Brotherhood of Anubis was no myth, and they were in New York.

NINE

"DON'T MOVE. I'm sending a car to pick you up." Decker had barely spoken the words before he was grabbing his coat and heading toward the door, car keys in hand.

He raced to his car, even as he was calling dispatch to get a cruiser over to Emma's location and bring her to the station. He could only hope that whoever broke into her apartment had given up after she fled. The attack was obviously connected to the statue and Daniel Montague's murder. Emma was lucky to be alive, and he wanted to make sure she stayed that way.

He peeled away from the curb, flicking on the blue lights concealed behind tinted glass at the front and rear of the unmarked unit, and weaved through the traffic toward the precinct.

When he arrived, Emma was already there, waiting in an interview room.

He entered and took a seat opposite her.

"Are you alright?"

"Yes." She nodded. "Your men picked me up a few minutes after I called you, thank goodness. I was so scared."

"I know." Decker noticed that Emma was shaking. He reached out and touched her hand, ever so lightly. He was about to speak again when he heard a low cough from the doorway.

He turned to find a uniformed officer standing there.

"I thought you might like an update," the cop said.

"Well?"

"We're conducting a search of the neighborhood, but so far there's no sign of the intruders. Looks like whoever the attackers were, they are long gone."

"Very good." Decker nodded. "What about the apartment?"

"Ransacked. There's no obvious sign of anything missing, but we can't know for sure. Maybe CSI will find something."

"It's a long shot," Decker said. "Let me know if you turn up any new leads."

"Yes, sir." The cop bowed his head and retreated.

Decker remained silent for a while, thinking, then turned to Emma. "You'll need to stay somewhere else until we catch the people who did this. You can't go back to your apartment. It's not safe."

"I'm not sure where else to go." Emma looked up at him, a worried expression on her face. "I work long hours, travel several months each year. It's hard to make friends."

"A work colleague, perhaps?" Decker asked.

"No." Emma looked unsure. "And even if there was, I don't want to endanger anyone else. Don't you guys have safe houses or something?"

"We do, but they are reserved for very specific circumstances. Witnesses in mob trials, that sort of thing. I'd never get clearance."

"I could check in to a hotel, I suppose."

"I don't think it's a good idea for you to be alone, given the circumstances," Decker said. He paused, thinking. "There is one other option. I have an extra bedroom at my place. You can stay there tonight."

"I don't want to impose."

"You're not," Decker said. "It's the safest place for you right now."

"If you're sure?"

"I am."

Emma nodded. "Alright, if you think that's best."

TEN

THE BLONDE-HAIRED, dark-skinned woman walked down the alley, her footsteps hurried, coat pulled up against the drizzle of rain that had descended upon the city. More than once she glanced backward, even though she knew she had not been followed. But it was always prudent to be careful.

She was angry.

Tonight's escapade had been a disaster, and worse, she had lost her face mask, allowed herself to be seen. The archaeologist woman wouldn't be able to identify her, she was sure, but still, it was sloppy.

Ahead was a steel door set into the rear of a nondescript brick building that had once been a commercial laundry. She approached and swiped a white keycard through a reader on the door frame.

A few moments passed, then there was a muffled click as hidden deadbolts released.

She pushed the door open and stepped inside. Making sure it closed again, she proceeded down a short corridor to a second door.

Now she paused, gathering her composure. She had been here many times, but on this visit she brought bad news, and she was unsure how that news would be met. A deep shame filled her. She had trained all her life for one singular purpose, and now that the moment was here, she was not up to the task. It was a humbling realization, and one she must admit to the person she admired most in the world.

But there was no point in delaying the inevitable.

It was time to face her failures. Admit to them. Own them.

With a deep breath, she opened the door and stepped into the room.

This space was nothing like the corridor from which she had entered. It was well appointed and opulent in its furnishings, with bookcases lining the walls and a fine Persian rug spread across the polished concrete floor. All around her were artifacts from every moment in Egyptian history, some small, others, like the stone statue of Isis that stood in the far corner, much larger. None of these objects were merely showpieces, however. They all held a special significance to the brotherhood. Unfortunately, the one object they craved, the one statue they needed, was still proving elusive.

"Selene, my dear." The voice came from a tall man sitting behind an ornate oak desk in the center of the room. "Please, come closer. Sit."

She took a step forward, then faltered.

"Sit." This time he barked the word in Arabic, his heavy accent hardly noticeable in his native tongue.

"As you wish." Selene crossed the room and sank into a high-backed chair facing the desk.

"I hear things did not go well this evening."

"No." Selene swallowed a lump of fear. "We ran into more resistance than we anticipated."

"If by resistance you mean one pathetic defenseless girl, then yes, you did." The man behind the desk observed her with a deadpan stare that sent a shiver up Selene's spine. And with good cause. This was the most powerful person in the order, the high priest of the Brotherhood of Anubis. Worse, he was her grandfather, and she had failed him. "I didn't raise you to be weak," he said.

"I'm sorry." She hung her head in shame, partly in deference to his standing, but mostly because she truly was ashamed.

"And then there was the debacle at the Montague mansion. So messy, and for what?"

"We had no reason to believe the statue would be so well hidden."

"You had no reason not to," her grandfather responded. "Montague knew you would be coming. He knew the importance of the Anubis statue. You failed to convince him of the futility of his situation."

"I wasn't the one–"

"I realize you didn't interrogate him personally. But you are the voice of my authority. You were there. The blame lies with you. He shouldn't have died until he told you where the statue was."

"I know."

"Selene." His voice softened, only for a moment. "You are my granddaughter and I love you, but this is bigger than either of us. Our family has guided the brotherhood for three millennia, watching, waiting, ever since the statue was lost to us. You know the prophecy. The statue will only reveal itself when the one true vessel walks the earth once more. It will draw them to it like a moth to the flame. Everything has fallen into place. The comet is returning, and that is the final sign. Soon Anubis will walk again, cloaked in the body of the chosen one, to judge all mankind. Only the worthy will be spared, and we will be among them."

"I know."

"But none of this can happen unless you complete your task."

"But the girl, are you sure?"

"Yes, my dear. The prophecy clearly states that Anubis will take female form in the next incarnation. There was only one female present when the statue was found. I am sure."

"I understand." Selene nodded. "I will make things right."

"Yes, you will." Her grandfather nodded. "Now go."

"As you wish." She turned to leave.

"Selene?" The old man spoke again.

"Yes?" She paused mid-stride, turning back toward him.

"I don't care what it takes, what you need to do. It is imperative that we have everything in place for the ceremony."

"I know."

"Good." The priest leaned back in his chair. "May Anubis guide you, my child."

"And you." Selene bowed and turned, making her way to the door. She walked along the corridor, her footfalls echoing as she went. Once outside, she leaned against the brick wall and composed herself. She felt foolish. Ashamed. But there was no time for self-pity. She must find the statue, and the girl. The only question was, how? For a while she stood there, thinking, even as the rain turned from a drizzle to a downpour and soaked through her clothing.

And then she had an idea.

With a renewed sense of purpose, Selene pulled her jacket tight, wiped the rainwater from her face, and started down the alley in the direction of the street beyond.

ELEVEN

THEY DROVE the short distance to Decker's apartment in silence. It wasn't until they were inside the building that Emma finally spoke again.

"I hope this isn't too much trouble."

"Not at all." Decker shook his head. "It's my job."

"I'm sure it isn't your job to babysit witnesses," Emma said.

"Don't worry about it," Decker replied. He led her through the apartment to the spare bedroom. "It's only a full-size bed, I'm afraid, but it's pretty comfortable."

"I'm sure it will be fine," Emma said. "Besides, I'm so tired I'd hardly notice if it were made of straw."

"I'll let you settle in," he said. "The bathroom is first on the right, and my bedroom is directly across the hall, so I'll be close at hand if you need me."

"Thank you, Detective Decker." Emma nodded.

"Call me John." Decker stood in the doorway, his hand resting on the handle. "Detective Decker is so formal."

"Alright. John it is." Emma smiled for the first time that evening. She sat on the bed.

Decker turned to leave, but then Emma spoke again.

"John?"

"Yes?" He turned back toward her.

"The people who attacked me tonight, I know who they are."

"Why didn't you say something earlier?" Decker stepped back into the room. "We would have known who to look for. We might have found them."

"I don't mean that I know who the actual people are by name," Emma said. "What I mean is, I know who sent those thugs to my apartment tonight, and what they wanted."

"The statue, obviously," Decker replied. "I should never have let you go home without putting a unit outside."

"It isn't your fault." Emma shook her head. "You had no idea they would come after me. I hadn't spoken to Daniel in years."

"Well, they did. We're lucky they didn't kill you."

"They tried." Emma's lip trembled when she said that, and Decker thought for a moment that she might start to cry, but then she pulled herself together and carried on. "I can't believe I escaped."

"You said you know who they are, the people who attacked you?"

"Yes. I pulled one of their masks off during the struggle. It was a woman."

"What?"

"There's more," Emma said. "She had a tattoo."

"So?" Decker shrugged. "Lots of people have tattoos."

"Not like this one." Emma met his gaze. "It's more like a mark. I've read about it in obscure texts, a jackal cartouche drawn on the neck of believers. It symbolizes the Brotherhood of Anubis."

"They're real, then."

"Yes."

"Something doesn't add up," Decker replied. "You said they're only rarely mentioned in old documents?"

"That's right, why?"

"It seems to me that any group that could survive that long would leave a bigger footprint on history. How did they keep going without people knowing about them?"

"The ancient Egyptians were very good at destroying the evidence of things they turned their back on. Look at the cult of Aten, the sun god. They almost wiped the evidence of that religion from the face of the Earth after the reign of Amenhotep III, who imposed his own cult on the public. Even Amarna, the city the Pharaoh built to immortalize the sun god, was destroyed and abandoned after his death."

"But the sun god cult didn't last all the way to the twenty-first century. It died out."

"True," Emma agreed. "But the Egyptians were also fanatical. I don't know how The Brotherhood of Anubis survived, but it did."

"There's one thing that I still don't understand."

"What?"

"Why this one statue in particular? Wouldn't any old Anubis statue do? There must be hundreds, even thousands of them, in museums and private collections all over the world."

"Not like this. It was linked to the pharaoh himself. It was made during his lifetime and buried with him upon death. With the mummy destroyed, the soul of the god will journey to the statue connected with him in life, where it will live until it can be transferred once again into a breathing host."

"You found the statue in the same place as the mummy that was destroyed in Cairo a few days ago." Decker filled in the blanks.

"Yes. It was the tomb of a little-known king, barely talked about in ancient writings. We excavated it and brought the mummy out along with that statue. Like I said before, the hiero-glyphics were most precise in their language. They laid out the process of resurrecting the god king. That's why the Brother-hood of Anubis are here now, at this moment in history." Emma took a long, measured breath. "They intend to bring the risen god of the underworld, Anubis, into this world, and they will kill anyone who gets in their way."

TWELVE

SELENE STEERED her BMW Roadster through the deserted early morning streets, driving a little under the speed limit despite the urge to do otherwise. She could not afford to attract the unwanted attention of a bored cop looking to write a speeding ticket.

She was still ashamed of her recent failures, and a little surprised that her grandfather had meted out punishment for her mistakes, but now she had a chance to put things right. First, she would find the statue, and then she would find the girl.

Her thoughts turned to Daniel Montague. He had died and taken his secrets with him to the afterlife, and that was where things started to go wrong. Despite many hours of excruciating torture, he never told them anything useful. When a search of his home turned up nothing, Selene assumed that the statue must be in the possession of the petite archeologist. That worked out well, since the girl was her next stop, anyway. But then the archeologist escaped, and a search of her apartment turned up nothing. Which meant the statue had probably been in Montague's house all along. They had merely failed to locate it.

But it wouldn't be there now, of that she was sure.

Worse, the spy she had left watching the girl's apartment reported that a policeman had taken her away in his car. There was only one explanation for that. The girl was in protective custody and out of reach, at least for now.

She turned left onto a narrow street, and then right, pulling up in front of a large stone building. She put the car into park and sat with the engine idling. After a few moments, she rolled down the driver's side window, ignoring the drops of rain that found their way into the vehicle, and peered up at the precinct house, and at the neat rows of police cars parked up outside. The statue was now inside that building, she felt certain. She must come up with a way to get it out, and soon.

THIRTEEN

EMMA WOKE to a stream of sunlight slanting in through a small window to the right of her bed. For a moment the unfamiliar surroundings confused her, but then the horrid events of the night before flooded back in full force. She lay there and stared at the ceiling, doing her best to ignore the feelings of panic that flared up when she thought about the break in.

After a while, the sound of footsteps outside her door announced that John Decker was awake and getting ready for work. She wondered if she should climb out of bed and talk to him before he left. It felt odd being in his house, and she was not sure what to do next, or where to go. She did not want to return to her apartment yet. Thinking about that caused a knot of fear that threatened to overwhelm her, yet she could not expect Decker to let her stay. It was enough that he had gone out of his way to protect her, and she did not wish to impose on him further.

It was while she was mulling over these conflicting emotions that there was a light knock at the bedroom door. Decker's voice filtered through from the other side.

"Emma?"

"Yes?" She hadn't noticed before, but his voice had a soft quality, almost soothing, with a slight southern drawl.

"Are you decent?" he asked. "Can I come in?"

"Of course." She sat up and pulled the covers to her chin to conceal her thin nightgown.

"I'm off to the precinct." Decker filled the doorway. "Will you be alright here on your own?"

"Sure." She nodded her head. "I'm a big girl."

"I know." Decker smiled, his eyes catching hers for a moment. "I wanted to make sure you were doing okay this morning. You had a tough time yesterday."

"I'm doing fine. Still a little shaken up, but nothing I can't handle."

"Good." Decker went to leave, then turned back to her. "By the way, I had a uniformed officer collect some clothes from your apartment. They are in a bag outside the door."

"Thank you so much." Emma had fled the apartment in nothing but her nightgown and coat. Until now, she hadn't thought about the fact that she had no clothing.

"You're welcome." Decker smiled and stepped into the hallway.

"John?"

"Yes?" He poked his head back into the room.

"It is okay if I stay here again tonight?" Emma felt a rush of embarrassment. "You can say no and I'll understand. It's just that..."

"You can stay as long as you want," Decker replied.

"Besides, you can't really go back to your apartment right now. It would be much too dangerous."

"Thank you," Emma said for a second time in as many minutes, relieved.

"My pleasure," Decker replied. "As long as you can put up with the place for a few days. It's hardly the Ritz."

"I've lived in tents in the desert, shared apartments in Cairo with a half dozen other sweaty archeologists and bunked down in huts that didn't even have running water. I think I can handle your spare bedroom for a few days."

"I will warn you though, I'm not a perfect roommate," Decker said, smiling. "I snore."

"Are you trying to put me off?"

"Not at all." Decker shook his head, grinning.

"Well, good, because it isn't working."

"I hear you," Decker said. "Just don't complain when the freight train from across the hall keeps you up all night."

"How do you know my snoring won't keep you up?"

"Touché." Decker grinned. "It's settled then?"

"Yes." She allowed herself a smile. She felt better knowing that that she could stay with John. He felt safe. Moreover, she felt safe around him.

"I'll be home as soon as I can this evening. I'll pick up pizza if you like. You like pizza?"

"Please." She stifled a snort. "Is the pope Catholic?"

"Pepperoni okay?"

"I'm looking forward to it already."

"Great. In the meantime, there's milk and eggs in the fridge, and cereal in the pantry. Help yourself to anything you can find."

"Thanks."

"You should stay inside today and keep a low profile. Don't go out and don't answer the door to anyone, understand?"

"Yes." Emma had no intention of answering the door after the events of the night before.

"Alright then. I'll see you later." Decker retreated, closing the door behind him.

Emma lay back and rested her head on the soft pillow. She listened as he puttered around for a few minutes, and then she heard the soft thud of the front door when he left. She stretched out and closed her eyes. She would get up soon and call the museum to let them know what had happened. But right now, the bed felt good, and she wanted to savor it for a while longer.

FOURTEEN

CONNOR WAS ALREADY at his desk when Decker arrived at the precinct.

"It's not like you to be late," Connor said. "Did you think it was your day off?"

"Very funny." Decker sat down. "Where are we on the Montague case? Did forensics come up with anything?"

"Nope. Nothing we don't already know," Connor replied.

"Damn."

"I heard about what happened last night. How's Emma?"

"A bit shaken up, but otherwise fine."

"Nasty business," Connor said. "I guess this confirms that Montague's killers were after the statue."

"It would appear so." Decker rubbed his temples. He was worried about Emma. She should be safe at his apartment, but that didn't make him feel any better. "The statue might be the key, but how does that help us?"

"I was thinking about that," Connor replied. "I came in early this morning and did some digging. I think you'll be interested in what I found."

"Well?" Decker leaned forward.

"I was wondering how the intruders traced the statue to the Montague mansion in the first place. It wasn't as if Daniel Montague advertised the fact that he had it. In fact, just the opposite. He smuggled it out of Egypt. Something like that, you keep quiet about."

"Agreed."

"So that leaves us with the question of how the killers knew it was there."

"An inside job," Decker said. "Someone who knew of Montague's dealings."

"I agree." Connor nodded. "It's the only way."

"I'm pretty sure Emma didn't tell anyone. So, who else knew the statue was in New York?" Decker said. "It must have been someone close to Montague, but he had no wife, no family to speak of. That leaves one of his team, a person he trusted."

"Which narrows it down."

"And he wouldn't have told his coworkers what he was planning. It would be too risky. The only reason Emma knew was because it was her excavation."

"If it wasn't one of the team in Egypt, that only leaves one option..."

"His importer," Decker said, realizing where Connor was heading. "There's no way Montague was packing artifacts into his suitcase. They would have been crated and sent via ship. That means there must have been someone on this end dealing with the import paperwork, making sure the shipments cleared customs."

"Bingo." Connor tapped a pile of paperwork on his desk.

"And I know who that was. Eastern Trade Import and Export Co. They're a small company running out of a warehouse near the docks. It's pretty much a one-man operation."

"Because Montague wouldn't trust a large outfit. Too much of a paper trail," Decker said.

"But a small company would fly under the radar," Connor chipped in. "It's much easier to get things done, be creative with the import papers, if you're only dealing with one person."

"And a small firm like that would be hungry enough for work to bend the rules, especially if Montague paid well."

"My thoughts exactly." Connor picked up a sheet of paper from his desk. "The guy who runs the company is one Amir Darzi. I ran a background check already. He was born in the USA to Israeli parents. There are a couple of old traffic tickets, but other than that, he has a clean record."

"We should talk to this guy, put some pressure on him. Maybe he can lead us to the killers."

"At the very least he might be able to give us something else to go on, because right now we're up against a brick wall."

"What are we waiting for?" Decker was already on his feet. "Let's pay a visit to Mr. Darzi and see what he can tell us."

FIFTEEN

BY NOON EMMA had made herself a cheese omelet, which she devoured in record time, and called the museum to say she would not be in for a few days. After that, she browsed the books piled high on a set of shelves in the living room. She ran her hand over the spines of several volumes, noting the eclectic mix of modern thrillers and classic works by authors as diverse as Mary Shelley and Charles Dickens. Many of the books were paperbacks. A few, mostly hard cover versions, looked older. She wondered if Decker had collected these or if they were passed on from a relative.

Either way, she had no intention of taking one of the collectible volumes, and in the end, she selected an adventure novel, which she took to a chair near the window. Decker had told her to keep a low profile, and anyone looking toward the apartment from the street might notice her sitting there, but she felt at ease near the window and liked being able to look out. Besides, if anyone suspicious came sniffing around, she would see them before they got to the front door, and that made her feel safer.

She read for two hours, but eventually grew weary and deposited the book on the windowsill.

She went to the kitchen and poured herself a glass of water. On the way back she paused beside a row of photographs arranged on the wall opposite the window.

There were four images in all, matted in black frames. The first contained a group of teenagers, one of whom she picked out as Decker right away. He must have been around sixteen when the shot was taken, and although he had grown older now, his face gaining the maturity of age, it was still easy to see the likeness. Next to him stood a pretty girl with long auburn hair, wearing a shirt that read Cassidy's Diner. They were grinning at the camera, arms around each other's waists. She wondered who the girl was. A first love, perhaps?

The next two photos were family portraits, a boyish Decker standing between his parents, freckle faced and grinning.

The final image was also Decker, wearing a fresh new police uniform. He looked young. Emma guessed he was in his early twenties. He was smiling, but something about the photo gave her the impression that the smile was for show. There was sadness in his eyes that poked through the mask of happiness. She studied the images for a while, trying to reconcile the joy she saw in the first three with the sadness that lurked behind the smile of the older Decker in the last one. Maybe she was wrong and was reading too much into the picture, but she could not shake the feeling that there was a cloud hanging over John Decker in that final photograph.

SIXTEEN

DECKER STEERED through the early afternoon traffic toward the warehouse Connor had discovered. When they arrived, Decker pulled into a parking space marked *Customer Parking Only* beside the only other vehicle on the lot, a battered van with the import company name on the side. They climbed from the car and walked toward the main entrance, skirting the van. Decker tugged on the front door.

It was locked.

A closed sign hung askew in the grimy window next to the door.

"That's odd." Decker tried the handle a second time to be sure.

"The place looks deserted." Connor cupped his hands and peered through the window. "No lights on inside. I guess he could have gone to breakfast."

"His van is still here," Decker said. "And there's nowhere to eat within walking distance."

"He might have a car. Maybe he only uses the van for work."

"Maybe." Decker stepped back and glanced around. The warehouse was a large brick building, the stonework painted white, although the paint had flaked away in several places to reveal the brickwork underneath. A row of filthy windows ran off to his right, secured by iron bars set in concrete sills. At the far end of the building was a roll-up door above a loading dock. The rest of the street was much the same, with rows of warehouse units stretching in both directions. On the other side of the road, between two dilapidated storage buildings, was a vacant lot full of weeds and trash. A broken concrete slab heaved up from the middle of the lot, cracked and slanted. "We can hang around a while, see if he comes back."

"Dammit." Connor turned and walked back toward the car. "Have you got anything to eat? I'm starving."

"There's a chocolate bar in the glove box. That's it."

"Better than nothing." Connor opened the passenger door. "If I knew we were going to end up on a stakeout, I'd have picked something up before we drove over here."

"Hang on a minute. We might be in luck." Decker watched a car turn onto the street from the main road and head toward them, slowing as it reached the warehouse. "Maybe this is our man."

"Let's hope so." Connor closed the door and rounded the car moments before an old, dented Mustang swung off the road and pulled up next to the van.

A tall, muscular man with a thin mustache and a shaved head exited his car. When he saw the two cops he froze, a look of confusion on his face.

"Are you Amir Darzi?" Decker asked, closing the gap

between them. He eyed the string of tattoos covering each of the man's arms.

"Amir?" The man shook his head. "Don't make me laugh. Do I look like that pot-bellied weasel?"

"We don't know. That's why we're asking." Connor came around from the other direction. "If you're not Amir Darzi, then who are you?"

"Name's Carlos," the man replied. "What's all this about, anyway? You two look like cops. You cops?"

"Homicide detectives," Decker said.

"Aw, shit." Carlos waved his arms. "Look, whatever business you have with Amir, I don't want to get involved."

"You got yourself involved by showing up." Decker rested his hand on his gun. "You clearly know Darzi. Why don't you tell us what you're doing here?"

"Look, I work for him once in a while, that's all. The man calls me when he needs help with a delivery, stuff he can't move on his own."

"He called you today?" Connor positioned himself between Carlos and the Mustang.

"Not today. Last week." Carlos backed up, casting his car a quick look. "He said he had a shipment that needed moving this morning and to get here around ten."

"Yeah, well, it looks like you made the trip for nothing," Decker said. "The place is locked up tight."

"Amir's not here?"

"That's what the man said." Connor leaned on the Mustang.

"He must be here." Carlos pointed. "That's his van right there."

"He doesn't have another vehicle?" Decker glanced at Connor.

"Amir?" Carlos snorted. "Are you kidding me? That skinflint? If his van's here, then he is."

"The locked door would say otherwise."

"He's in there. There's no way he'd miss a delivery." Carlos removed a cell phone from his pocket. "I'll prove it to you." He lifted the phone to his ear. A moment later he canceled the call, a puzzled expression on his face. "He's not answering."

"Are you calling a landline or a cell phone?"

"Cell phone."

"Dial the number again," Decker said.

"Why?"

"Just do it." Decker went back to the locked door and leaned in close. From somewhere inside the building he heard the faint sound of a jangling musical ringtone. He stepped back. "Darzi might not be answering, but his phone's in there, for sure."

"Are you thinking what I'm thinking?" Connor pushed himself up from the Mustang and made his way over to the door.

"Darzi's van is here. His cell phone is here," Decker said. "Yet the building is locked up tight and all the lights are off. Something's not right."

"Agreed," Connor said. "Do we have enough to warrant breaking the lock?"

"I think we might," Decker replied.

"Then let's do it," Connor said. "I'll get the crowbar from the car."

SEVENTEEN

THE DOOR CRASHED BACK on its hinges, hitting the wall. Decker glanced at Connor, who stood wielding a bright yellow crowbar, and then stepped across the threshold into the dark warehouse.

He found a light switch and clicked it on to reveal a small reception room with a dusty metal desk in one corner and two doors leading in opposite directions.

The door on the right had the word WAREHOUSE stenciled on it, while the one to the left stood open, revealing a small corridor, off which were several more doors.

Decker paused for a moment, listening, and then called out. "Hello? Mr. Darzi? This is the police."

Silence greeted him in reply.

"Maybe he's shy." Connor stepped into the room, followed by Carlos.

"Or maybe he doesn't like cops." Decker made his way to

the warehouse door and opened it, poking his head inside. It was dark, but he could see the outlines of several crates.

"Where's Darzi's office?" Connor asked, turning to Carlos.

"This way." Carlos took off along the corridor, passing two doors before stopping at the third. "In here."

"Mr. Darzi?" Decker called through the door, though he held out little hope of a response. "We're coming in, okay?"

They waited a moment, and then Decker gripped the handle and pushed the door inward. At the same time the air inside the room escaped, carrying with it a sulfur-laced odor that burned the nostrils.

Decker recognized it right away.

It was the stench of death.

"Shit." Connor glanced at Decker. "After you."

"Thanks." Decker stepped into the office, with Connor following behind.

The room was small, containing a desk and two bookcases, both crammed with papers. But it was the corpse sitting behind the desk, the skin already yellow and bloated in the humid atmosphere of the warehouse, which stopped the two policemen in their tracks. His wrists were tied to the chair with duct tape, and his shirt was pulled open, revealing a torso crisscrossed with deep, bloody lacerations. To his horror, Decker noticed that all of Darzi's fingernails were heaped in a pile on the desk in front of him, the roots dark crimson.

"I think we've found Amir Darzi," Connor said. "No wonder he didn't answer his phone. Poor guy must have been like this for days."

"Yeah." Decker looked at the corpse, a shudder running through him.

"Looks like the same people that killed Montague," Connor said.

"Without a doubt," Decker agreed. "They tortured this guy into giving up Montague's address. He must have told them the statue would be there."

"And once they got what they needed, they finished him off." Connor examined the small round hole in Darzi's forehead, and the trickle of blood crusted underneath.

"They executed him." Decker stepped away, into the corridor, no longer wishing to see the grisly contents of the office. "We'd better call this in."

EIGHTEEN

DECKER ARRIVED BACK at the apartment a little after nine, pizza in hand. He looked weary. Emma sensed that his day had not gone well. She wanted to ask him about it, but could not find the right words, and he didn't offer any information. In the end, she made small talk until they settled at the kitchen table to eat. It was then that Decker finally let the conversation turn to the afternoon's events.

"We visited an importer Daniel Montague used to bring shipments into the country," Decker said between mouthfuls of pizza. "We think that's how the killers found him."

"Daniel used a few different import companies," Emma replied. "Depending on what he was having shipped."

"This was a one-man outfit in Brooklyn. Eastern Trade Import and Export Co." Decker took another slice. "Ever heard of it?"

"Yes." Emma felt a tingle of apprehension. "Daniel used them several years ago to bring some papyrus into the country.

The guy that ran it was odd, and not in a good way. He made my skin crawl."

"Amir Darzi."

"That's him." Emma remembered how she felt when she first met Darzi, the way he looked at her with beady, black eyes. "Horrible little man. I didn't like him. He had a reputation."

"What kind of reputation?"

"For getting things done without drawing unwanted attention. Cutting corners, filing false papers. Using back door methods to bring in shipments."

"Smuggling."

"If you like. I didn't want to be associated with such shady tactics. I told Daniel as much," Emma said. "He promised not to use him again."

"Well, he did. It appears he hired Eastern Trade Imports to move the statue of Anubis out of Egypt. Connor found the import records among the documents in his study. They list several artifacts of little interest. There's no mention of the statue, naturally, but we're sure that's how it arrived in the country."

"What did Mr. Darzi have to say?" Emma asked.

"Not so much. He'd been dead for days." Decker toyed with his slice of pizza. "He was tortured, no doubt to get him to give up information on Daniel Montague and where his shipments were delivered."

"That's awful."

"Once they found what they wanted, they finished him off with a bullet to the head."

"Oh." Emma felt a sudden pang of sadness. She choked up. "If Daniel hadn't been so stubborn, if he'd only listened to me, he would still be alive."

"Most likely," Decker said. "But he made his decision. You can't change the past, even if you want to. It's better to let it go. Trust me, I've been there."

"Really?" Emma wiped away a tear. She felt embarrassed, weeping in front of Decker.

"Yes." He reached out, took her hand in his. "I know what it's like to wish you could go back and do things differently. Guilt is a terrible thing to live with."

"What happened?" Emma was aware of Decker's hand squeezing hers, but she made no move to withdraw it. He made her feel safe.

"It was a long time ago."

"I'm sorry. I didn't mean to pry," she said quickly. "You don't have to tell me."

"I don't mind." Decker glanced toward the wall and the row of pictures. "My mother was murdered when I was a young boy. She was killed in the woods outside of town. I was so young - I didn't understand what had happened. For the longest time I thought it was my fault, that she left because she didn't love me."

"That's so sad," Emma said. "What about your father? He must have been there for you."

"My father took it hard. After she died, he became withdrawn. He was obsessed with finding her killer. He was the town sheriff, you see. He thought he should have been able to protect her, and since he couldn't do that, the next best thing was to find out why she had died."

"I can understand that."

"Me too. The problem was, he couldn't focus on anything else. He paid scant attention to me, acted like I was an inconvenience. Eventually it was like I wasn't there at all."

"It must have been horrible."

"It was. If it wasn't for…" Decker's words trailed off, his eyes lingering on one photograph, the one with the pretty girl in it.

Emma watched him for a moment and then spoke up. "A girlfriend?"

"Nancy Cassidy. Her family ran the local diner, probably still does. We met in school and dated all through my senior year. I loved her so much. She loved me too."

"So why aren't you with her?" Emma was aware that she was stepping over a line, but she could not help herself. "What happened?"

"I was angry, stupid." Decker shook his head. "The minute I was old enough, I took off. I left everything behind, my father, Nancy, that town. I couldn't stand to be there one more second. Nancy was only a junior. She still had another year of school before she would graduate. I thought that I could run away from my demons. I went to college, then moved to New York, and joined the police. The rest is history, as they say."

"I see."

"The funny thing is, I despised my father. As the years went on and he became more and more lost in his own personal hell, I came to loath him. He passed away a few years ago, having never found my mother's killer. Funny that I should choose to follow in his footsteps and join the force."

"Not really, you seem to be an excellent cop. You clearly found your calling," Emma said. "What about Nancy? Have you spoken to her since?"

Decker shook his head. "I wouldn't know where to begin. I betrayed her, left her behind in that town. I didn't wait, even though I'd promised to. I can't imagine she would ever want to see me again."

"You could try."

"It's ancient history." Decker rose to his feet and scooped up the pizza box. He dumped it in the trashcan. "I'm sorry. I didn't mean to bend your ear. I was supposed to be making you feel better, not unloading my personal demons on you."

"You have made me feel better." Emma stood and closed the gap between them. "You've been nothing but wonderful through all of this. I don't know what I would have done without you."

"I'm just doing my job. That's all."

"Seems like you've gone above and beyond your job description over the last few days. I can't imagine your partner, Connor, letting me crash at his place."

"You wouldn't want to crash there, anyway. Connor's place is always a disaster. Trust me," Decker said, his face relaxing a little. "Empty fast food containers, beer bottles, and dirty clothes everywhere." He turned to her. "Enough of this maudlin talk. I think we need a distraction."

"What do you have in mind?"

"There's a bottle of Chardonnay chilling in the fridge. How about we break that sucker open and see where we go from there?"

"Sounds great." Emma grinned.

"Perfect." Decker opened the fridge and handed her the bottle. "I'll find a couple of glasses and meet you in the living room."

NINETEEN

A CRESCENT MOON hung over the city, low and milky white. For the second time in two days Selene drove through the empty late-night streets, enjoying the purr of the powerful BMW engine under her foot. Last night she had felt awful. But not now. Instead, she was focused and alert. She had spent the day formulating a plan to obtain the statue, which she was about to put into action. From now on, everything would fall into place, she was sure.

A parking garage loomed up ahead, the multi-story structure nestled between tall skyscrapers. Come morning there would be thousands of cars parked here, their owners working in the offices and stores close by, but at this time of night it was deserted, which was why she had selected it.

She pulled up to the entrance, took a ticket, and waited for the guardrail to rise. When it did, she edged forward and drove past the empty bays on the ground floor, ignoring them. There were only a few cars here, but she did not want to risk being seen, which was why she kept going until she reached the top floor. No one would venture this far into the garage with so many available spaces on the levels below, and even better, the open-air top floor had no security cameras.

She stopped, the car straddling two spaces with the front of the vehicle pointing toward the exit. This gave her an escape route if needed. It always paid to be careful.

She glanced at her watch.

11:55pm.

She was five minutes early.

Selene rested her head back and relaxed, keeping an eye on the ramp. A few minutes passed, and then she saw the twin beams of headlights piercing the darkness. A few moments later, a car appeared.

She sat back up, alert now.

The car approached, slowing to a stop ten feet away. Her hand fell to the gun she kept in the door pocket next to her seat. A second pistol, pushed into her waistband at the small of her back, would be within easy reach once she exited the vehicle, should things go south.

The new arrival sat awhile, engine rumbling, probably summing up the situation, and then the headlights snapped off and the car fell silent.

The driver's side door opened, and someone stepped out. Selene watched until she was satisfied that this was the person she was here to meet, and then she opened her own door and climbed from the car.

She kept her arms at her sides, palms flat. If needed, she could have the gun out and ready in less than a second. No doubt the person standing across from her was equally cautious, his own gun within easy reach. If all went well, neither would need them.

She moved toward him, and soon they stood facing each other a few feet apart.

"You came alone?" Her hand flexed, ready to go for the gun if this was a trap.

"Naturally," the man replied. "You?"

"Yes."

"Good." He seemed to relax a little. "Now let's get to the business at hand. I don't want to be here any longer than necessary."

"Agreed." Selene met his gaze. "Tell me about the statue. Do you know where it is?"

"Yes, and I can get it for you." The man shifted position. "For the right price, of course."

"Good." Selene smiled. "But there's one more thing. I want the girl too."

"That might be difficult."

"Find a way."

"It will cost more," the man said. "Quite a lot more."

"I guessed as much," Selene replied. "I'm sure we can come to an arrangement."

"What do you want with her?"

"That's none of your business."

"Fair enough." The man nodded. "All we need to do now is agree on my payment."

TWENTY

AT MIDNIGHT, her head spinning from two glasses of wine, Emma slipped between the sheets. She closed her eyes and let out a sigh. Things might be all messed up, but right here, right now, she felt pretty good, although she suspected it was the alcohol taking effect. Either way, she would accept it. A week ago, she was on a dig halfway around the world, pulling artifacts from the sand, studying them, cataloguing them, and now she was hiding from a murderous cult in a cop's apartment.

From somewhere beyond her door, the sound of a toilet flushing drew her back to reality. Decker was preparing for bed. She wondered why he didn't have a wife or a girlfriend. Sure, he'd had a tough life, but he was a good-looking guy, and he seemed nice. Not that she could say much. She'd only been on three dates in the last two years, and nothing had come of any of them. It didn't help that she was a workaholic, or that she was always overseas in some remote part of the world. Sometimes she wondered if her job intimidated men. It didn't matter. She was happy the way she was. Still, it would be nice to have some romance in her life once in a while.

Maybe once all this was over, she would see if Decker wanted to go out for a drink. She had a feeling he was not intimidated by anything. She smiled at that thought, a warm, fuzzy feeling enveloping her. She pulled the sheets up to her chin and pushed her head deep into the pillows.

She closed her eyes, the week's events heavy on her mind. She wished they had never unearthed the statue. It had caused so much trouble. Daniel was dead, and she was hiding from his killers, fearful for her own life. As she lay there, thinking, her mind drifted back to that long-ago day in the scorching Egyptian sands, when she had first laid eyes on the statue of Anubis. The day that started this whole nightmarish sequence of events in motion…

TWENTY-ONE

EGYPT—SEVERAL *years earlier*

The Valley of the Kings basked in the golden glow of the early morning sun, which was already warming the dry desert air to a stifling ninety-five degrees. By early afternoon it would be at least fifteen degrees hotter, turning the land into a parched hell, but for now it was bearable.

Emma Wilson stood on a rocky outcrop and observed the rising cliffs that stretched away to the horizon, the valley a deep cleft running between them. The rugged beauty of this place always amazed her, and sometimes she wondered if she was more at home here, in the vast Egyptian wilderness, than in the noisy metropolis of New York.

She shifted position, picking her way over to the trail that led back to the dig site, careful not to lose her footing. Fifty feet below, near the base of a craggy hill, she could make out the bustle of workers as they cleared away sand and uncovered the ruins beneath. The white of their garments, the long, almost floor length shirts called gallibaya that kept the locals much cooler than those wearing Western attire, stood out in stark contrast to the ochre desert floor. She watched the activity for a moment, and then her eyes wandered further afield to the row of tents beyond the dig. Here they ate and slept, sorted through the smaller relics, and huddled around campfires for warmth when the temperature dropped at night. She spied a solitary figure lingering beside one of the tents, his identity unmistakable thanks to the neat pressed trousers and jacket he wore despite his surroundings.

Daniel Montague.

As usual, he was up early, ready to oversee the day's work.

She stepped onto the loose shingle, negotiating the narrow trail back to the camp, careful of her footfalls. A slip here might not be fatal, but it would not be good.

Soon the meandering path leveled out to flatter ground, and she headed in the direction of the tents, intent upon freshening up before going to the dig site.

As she approached, Daniel spotted her, and a grin spread across his weathered face. "Emma, my dear. Out for your morning walk, I see."

"As always." She smiled and stepped between the tents. "It clears my head. Sets me up for the day."

"You must be careful not to step on a scorpion up there. A sting would be inconvenient, not to mention dangerous."

"I'm fine. This isn't my first time, you know," Emma laughed. If anything, Daniel was the rookie. While she had been on at least a dozen expeditions to this part of the world, this was only his fourth, and he wasn't even trained. But a bank account brimming with cash pulled a lot of strings, and an insatiable appetite for anything Egyptian meant there was no way he was funding a dig he didn't get to go on, so here he was. Regardless, he had proven himself to be a fine amateur archeologist, and he was a swift learner.

"I know, my dear, but I can still worry, can't I?" He rested a hand on her shoulder. "After all the adventures we've been through, you are like a daughter to me."

"I appreciate that." Emma nodded. She was about to continue when a rising chatter of excitement from the direction of the dig site drew her attention. "What's going on there?"

The site foreman, a tall, lean man with short, dark hair and olive skin, approached, his eyes wide. He spoke in a thick accent, his words hurried and quick. "Miss Wilson, Mister Montague, you must come quickly. I must show you."

"What is it, Akram?" Daniel asked the man. "What have you found?"

"A room, sir." Akram pointed toward the dig. "A new room. You will see."

"A new chamber?" Emma raised an eyebrow. "I thought we weren't venturing further into the tomb until everything in the outer chambers has been catalogued."

"The back wall," Akram said. "We were clearing sand, and it fell. There is another room behind."

"Come on." Daniel was already moving, following Akram back toward the excavation. "I want to see this."

"Wait." Emma paused for a moment, then let out a sigh before running to catch up. "We should wait."

"Why?" Daniel was already at the entrance to the tomb. He ducked under the mighty stone plinth holding the sands back and descended a set of steep steps. He navigated the narrow corridor leading to the first room, a large antechamber used to store offerings for the king's journey into the afterlife. Many of the relics from this room had been removed for cataloguing and study, but some still remained. Ancient jars of food and wine lined one wall, and next to that, the wheels and carriage of a chariot, too big to easily remove. "This is what we came here to do."

"We have to make sure the area is safe, that there won't be any further collapse."

"It's fine. We've already surveyed the tomb for structural integrity."

"That was before a wall came down." Emma was breathing hard. She stopped to catch her breath, noting how the air in the tomb was several degrees cooler than outside. It made sense. They were sixty feet inside a hill that jutted from the side of the valley. The chamber she now stood in had been hewn out by hand thousands of years before, a gargantuan effort no doubt, but just another normal day for the people who had built this place.

"You worry too much." Daniel took a step forward, approaching the dark hole that yawned before them, the light from the industrial lamps set up in the antechamber unable to penetrate the gloom beyond. He paused at the entrance. "You should go first. It's your expedition."

"I still think we should hold off, at least until the ceiling is propped up."

"That ceiling has been there for thousands of years, it's not going anywhere in the next few hours." Daniel nudged her forward. "Go on."

"Well…" She wanted to resist, but the urge to peek inside the newly discovered space was overwhelming. Even so, she was the head of the expedition. She should exercise restraint. On the other hand, the room was there, waiting for them to explore. It would be foolish not to take the opportunity.

"We're here now. You might as well go inside." It was as if Daniel had read her mind. "You can't make history if you don't take risks."

"You know, you're right." Emma cast a quick glance toward the roof of the tomb to reassure herself that it was stable, took a deep breath, and stepped across the threshold.

At first, she didn't see anything, but then, as she cast her flashlight around, she gasped. The room was filled with magnificent objects. Gold glinted under the beam of her flashlight, and everywhere she saw marvels. In the center of the room, on a stone dais, sat a beautifully preserved sarcophagus, still sealed. But it was what stood at the head of the sarcophagus that made her shake with excitement. There, on a stone pedestal covered in hieroglyphics, stood a statue so perfect it might be the best example ever found. She crept forward in awe, closing the distance between herself and the object.

She heard Daniel enter, following behind. When he spoke, his words were soft and reverent. "This is incredible."

"Yes, it is," she agreed, never taking her eyes from the statue.

Daniel drew level and stared up at the statue. "Do you recognize who this is?"

"I do," Emma said in hushed tones, reaching out to touch it even though she knew it was a breach of protocol, but she was unable to resist. When her hand made contact with the statue, she felt a jolt of energy run from her fingers and up the length of her arm, almost like the object was electrified.

"Well?" Daniel urged.

"It's Anubis, the god of the underworld." Emma drew her hand away, rubbing it, unsure what had happened. "And it's wonderful."

TWENTY-TWO

THE COOL NIGHT air rustled the flaps of the tent, sending the loose canvas back and forth against itself. Most nights, the air was still and flat in the valley, but not tonight. It was almost as if the valley itself were mad at the interference of the archeologists, thought Emma as she lay on her cot and stared up at the fabric roof of her shelter.

She closed her eyes, listening to the gentle fingers of wind, but then, out in the camp, she heard something else.

A footfall.

She froze, her ears straining. Ordinarily there would be nothing sinister about someone walking around the camp at night. Perhaps they were heading for the latrine or sneaking off to grab a quick smoke, but she didn't think so. The sound was different, deliberately subdued, and it concerned her. After so many nights sleeping out in the desert, she had grown accustomed to the usual noises of the camp, and this was wrong. It was too furtive, as if the person was trying to hide their passage.

She sat up, reached for her clothes, slipped into them as quickly as she could, and then crawled to the front of the tent.

She pulled back the flaps, careful not to make a noise, and peered out.

Everything was still and quiet.

For a moment she wondered if she had imagined the sounds, but then there was a flicker of movement on the far side of the camp. It was barely visible, no more than a shift in the blackness of night, but she knew what she had seen. Worse, it was in an area of the camp that should be empty right now, near the tent that held the newly discovered artifacts. She could think of no reason why someone would legitimately be there.

Thoughts of grave robbers filled her head, relic hunters out to loot what they could from the ancient tombs and sell their ill-gotten gains on the black market. The theft of valuable antiquities was a huge problem, but rarely were the thieves brazen enough to actually infiltrate a working dig.

She glanced over at the other tents, where the rest of the team lay sleeping. Further back, obscured from her view, was another row of tents housing the local laborers, the men hired to clear away the sands and lift the rocks.

None of these people would be of any use. By the time she woke them, the thieves would be gone. There was only one thing to do.

She reached back inside the tent and drew out the hunting knife she kept under a pile of clothes, then slipped outside.

She stood and waited, listening, but the night was calm, serene. Her heart beating fast in her chest, Emma moved off, crossing the space until she was close to the spot where she had seen the movement.

Holding the knife tight in her hand, she went to the tent housing the artifacts retrieved from the tomb and lifted the flap.

It was dark inside the tent, the only illumination coming from a battery-powered LED lantern hanging from an overhead pole. This light stayed on at all times to ensure no one tripped on a priceless relic or kicked a canopic jar and broke it. During the day, when sunlight filtered into the tent, it was adequate. Now, in the pitch-black darkness of the night, its illumination struggled to reach the four corners of the tent beyond the stacks of crated objects waiting to be shipped off to either New York or the Cairo Museum for further study. Yet more artifacts were waiting to be catalogued and photographed. These were stored near the back, where tables had been set up to examine them.

It was in this section that Emma saw the figure.

He was thickset, bulky, wearing black from head to toe. Emma could not make out any facial features, thanks in part to the gloom, but also because of the dark bandana he wore across his face, leaving only his eyes visible. What she did see, though, was the object cradled in his arms. The statue of Anubis retrieved from the burial chamber that very morning.

A lump caught in her throat.

She felt a sudden flash of indecision.

In hindsight, it had been foolish not to awaken Daniel and the others. Now she was facing this thief alone and armed only with a small hunting knife. But at least she had that much.

She gripped the handle tight and stood her ground, meeting the intruder's gaze with as much defiance as she could muster.

They remained locked in a stalemate, with Emma blocking the only route out of the tent. Then, with a fluidity that surprised her, the intruder ducked sideways behind a stack of shipping crates and was lost from view.

She hesitated, her sense of self-preservation kicking in once again. If she went back now and roused the others from sleep, there would be safety in numbers. But the intruder had the statue of Anubis, and there was no telling how far away he would be by the time she returned with reinforcements. In the end, she came to the same conclusion as before. She must follow the thief, and even if she could not recover the statue, she might be able to see where he went, which would make finding the statue later much easier.

Decision made, she hurried through the tent toward the place the intruder had ducked out of sight. When she arrived, she found a gaping hole cut in the canvas wall, the ragged edges catching in the wind.

He had escaped, after all.

Emma pulled the ripped fabric aside and stepped through, shivering as the cold night air swirled around her.

She searched for the thief, but there was no sign of anyone. What she did see were footprints in the sand, leading away from camp toward a narrow ravine.

She mustered all her courage and followed.

Her heart was racing, and her breath came in short bursts. Her lungs protested the unusually harsh workout, but she pushed ahead until she came to a turn in the rocks that led to a wide, open space surrounded by low hills.

It was then that she saw her quarry once more, his form silhouetted against the moonlit sand as he hurried away with his precious cargo, cradled it like a newborn baby.

"Hey," she called out, the sound echoing through the valley. "Stop."

The thief must have heard her because he slowed and

glanced over his shoulder, clearly surprised that she was still in pursuit.

"Come back here." Emma did not know what she would do if he complied, but at least she still had the knife, which made her feel a little safer.

"I don't think so." The thief's voice was heavily accented, and Emma felt a sudden twinge of recognition, but she could not think why.

"Please, don't take the statue," Emma pleaded.

"Anubis is ours," the intruder replied, raising his voice above the desert wind. "We must fulfill its destiny."

"What does that mean?" Emma could feel a growing tightness in her legs as she worked to navigate the shifting sands. She would not be able to go on much longer at this pace.

"Do not try to follow me." The thief was slowing too, clearly finding the floor of the ravine as difficult as she was. He stumbled ahead, his footfalls careless and hurried, and then he fell.

Emma cried out, barely able to watch as the thief took a hand from the statue to steady himself. If it fell from his grip it might get damaged, chipped on a rock, or worse, shattered into a hundred pieces. She wanted to shout out to him again, tell him to be careful, but at that very moment, she felt the earth rumble beneath her.

The sudden movement took her by surprise. She came to a halt, wondering what was happening.

The rumble turned to a deafening roar.

The ground trembled.

Emma wondered if this might be an earthquake. There had been quakes in this region before. But then she saw the ground in front of the thief, or rather the lack of it, and she knew this was no ordinary event.

Where the valley floor had been, there was now a chasm twenty feet across and growing. Sand poured over the rim into the abyss, along with rocks and the sparse vegetation that clung to the desert floor.

The thief wasn't running now. He was watching the ground fall away in horror; the edge creeping closer and closer. He turned toward her, his bandana dislodged and hanging low over his neck, and in that moment, Emma recognized the thief. It was Akram, the foreman who oversaw the local work crews.

She also recognized something else.

Fear.

As the edge of the hole reached him, and the ground fell out from under his feet, his eyes widened in terror. And then, with a final, gut-wrenching scream, he was gone, lost to the void.

"No," Emma wailed, more concerned for the statue than for the man who had stolen it. She stepped toward the ever-expanding hole, hoping that the statue had not followed Akram into the pit, but she knew that it had.

And then, as she searched the widening gulf, she was overcome with a sense of someone watching her. She lifted her head and saw why.

There, standing across from her on the other side of the pit, was a lone figure.

Emma stood transfixed.

The figure spoke, and she recognized the voice as Daniel Montague, only it wasn't the Daniel she had left sleeping back at the camp. This was another Daniel. He looked older, and he looked tired.

She struggled to comprehend this thought. How could there be two Daniels? It didn't make any sense.

Only it did, and she knew why.

She must have fallen asleep while thinking about the dig and somehow woven the fabric of her thoughts into a dream.

"Emma." Daniel's voice was commanding.

"Yes?" She focused her attention back on him.

"I was wrong to take the statue." Daniel's voice was soft now. Repentant. "It holds too much power."

"I don't understand." Emma wondered how she could hear Daniel despite the distance between them, but she could. It was like his words were forming in her head.

"You must protect it. Don't let them take it."

"The statue is safe. It's locked away where no-one can get to it," she said.

"No." Daniel shook his head. "It is not safe."

"Yes, it is."

"They will keep coming," Daniel said. "They will never stop looking."

"Who?" Emma asked, even though she knew the answer - The Brotherhood of Anubis.

"You must protect the statue." Daniel was fading now, his form becoming opaque. "You are the only one who can."

"Wait. I don't understand." She could see the desert coming into view behind him as he faded away.

"Anubis has chosen you." The words were faint, as if coming from a long way off. "Tread carefully, Emma."

And now, as Daniel disappeared entirely, the ground rumbled and shook, heaving up in places, and down in others. Cracks snaked out from the edge of the hole, weaving their way toward her. She turned to run, but the chasm was growing faster than she could move, and soon there was nothing underfoot but air, and then she was falling into the void, even as a terrified scream escaped her lips.

TWENTY-THREE

DECKER HEARD the scream and snapped awake.

He sprang from the bed and grabbed his gun from the nightstand, then sprinted to the bedroom door, holding the gun at the ready as he entered the corridor.

He listened for a moment, straining to hear any unusual sound, but there was nothing. If there were intruders in the house, they were doing a good job of keeping quiet.

Satisfied that he was not in immediate danger, Decker moved toward the spare bedroom. When he swung the door open, Emma was sitting in the dark, illuminated only by the soft yellow glow of the streetlamp outside. She was frozen in place; the bed covers bunched up around her legs. Her hair was matted, a thin sheen of sweat coated her forehead, and her chest heaved as she drew in long breaths. She looked scared to death.

"What's wrong?" He stepped into the room.

"A bad dream, that's all." There was a tremble to her voice.

"When you screamed, I thought the people who attacked you had found us."

"Sorry," Emma said. "I didn't mean to scare you."

"That's okay." Decker sat on the edge of the bed. "What were you dreaming about, the assault in your apartment?"

"No." Emma shook her head. "I was thinking about Egypt, and the day we found the statue. I must have fallen asleep."

"Do you want to tell me about it?" Decker asked.

"I don't want to bother you. It was unsettling, that's all."

"My mother always said that speaking a nightmare robbed it of its power," Decker said. "If you talk about it, you will feel better. I promise."

"Okay. But stop me at any time if it gets too boring," Emma said. "It was about two weeks into the expedition when a wall collapsed in the tomb we were excavating. Beyond it was a burial chamber full of wonderful things. Figurines, carvings, papyrus, all sorts of stuff stacked there for millennia. That's where we found Anubis, sitting high on a dais overlooking the sarcophagus of the king. That night, our foreman, Akram, tried to steal the statue while we slept. I caught him in the tent where we housed the newly discovered items. He claimed he was checking on it, making sure it was safe, but that was a lie. He had it in a duffel bag wrapped in cloth. Daniel was furious and fired him on the spot. At the time we were baffled by his behavior. He was such a good worker. Loyal. At least so we thought. We figured he was going to sell the statue on the black market, but now…"

"You think he was working for the same people that killed Daniel and attacked you."

"Maybe," Emma replied. "He might have been a spy, put there by the Brotherhood of Anubis."

"So that was the whole dream?"

"No." Emma wiped a hand across her forehead, pushing some stray hairs away. "The dream was different. Akram took the statue and ran. I gave chase, and things got really weird. Before I could catch him, a chasm opened up and swallowed him, and then I saw Daniel. He talked to me."

"What did he say?" Decker wondered if the events of the last few days had affected her more than she realized.

"That the statue needed to be protected, that it holds some sort of power."

"That makes sense." Decker moved closer to her on the bed. He reached out and took her hand in his. "Daniel was killed for that statue. You were attacked. There's a fanatical cult looking for it, and you said yourself that the ancient Egyptians believed the statue to have magical qualities. It makes sense that you would weave those things into your dream. It was all in your head, nothing more."

"But Daniel spoke to me." Tears welled in her eyes.

"No, he didn't." Decker's voice was soft, gentle. "Daniel is dead."

"I know it makes no sense, but it all felt so real, even the stuff that I know never happened in real life, like the chasm."

"Dreams can feel real sometimes," Decker said.

"I know." Emma forced a smile. "I shouldn't be getting emotional like this. I'm a practical, grounded archeologist, after all."

"You've had a tough couple of days."

"I'm alright now though." Emma let her head fall back on the pillow.

Decker let her hand go and stood. "I'll let you get back to sleep. I'm just next door if you need me."

"Don't leave." Emma reached up and took his hand again. She pulled him back to the bed.

"Emma…"

"Please. I don't want to be alone right now. Stay with me tonight." Her eyes were wide, imploring. "I'm scared."

"Alright." Decker wondered if he was stepping over a line, but he hadn't the heart to leave. He nodded toward the chair in the corner of the room. "I can sleep there if it makes you feel better."

"No." Emma pushed the covers aside. "Hold me."

Decker hesitated a moment, then laid down next to Emma. She lifted the covers over them and scooted close until her body was pressed against his, head resting on his shoulder. Her hair smelled like freshly cut flowers. He could feel the gentle rise and fall of her chest against him as he put his arm around her, holding her. He stroked her hair, the movements slow and gentle, and watched in the darkness until she fell asleep. Even then, he watched her some more, until his own eyes grew heavy, and sleep finally found him too.

TWENTY-FOUR

THE NEXT MORNING, they drove across town in silence. Neither one mentioned the night before, nor how they had slept in each other's arms until dawn, when Decker arose and made steaming cups of coffee as the first rays of the sun slanted through his kitchen window. Emma was still disturbed by the nightmare, but she did not say anything. Maybe Decker was right, and it was all in her head, her mind dredging up past memories, but then again, maybe not. It all felt so real, even the parts she knew had not actually happened, and it left her with a strange feeling that she could not shake, that the spirit of Daniel had reached out from beyond the grave and actually talked to her. It was crazy, of course. Things like that did not happen, and she was a rational person, but still, she was left pondering, and by the time they arrived at the precinct, she felt no different. When Decker pulled into the parking lot, she was happy to escape the car and focus on something else.

They made their way inside the building and rode up the

elevator to the second floor where the homicide division was housed and headed toward Decker's desk.

Detective Connor was nowhere in sight.

"That's odd." Decker glanced around before noticing a hand-written note sitting next to his laptop.

He opened it, frowning.

Emma peered over his shoulder to read the note.

Following up on a lead. Will be back later.
Connor

"Looks like it's the two of us," Decker said, crumpling the note and tossing it into the wastebasket.

"Great," Emma replied, a little too enthusiastically. She looked sheepish. "I mean…"

"It's alright. I get it." Decker smiled. "Connor can be a little brusque at times."

"He is a bit abrupt." She bit her bottom lip. "Since Connor isn't here, can we look at the statue again? I'd like to reassure myself that it's safe."

"The evidence locker is as good as a bank vault, trust me."

"I know. But even so…" Her mind drifted back to the nightmare, to Akram running through the desert, and Daniel's words. Besides, she was certain there was more to the statue than met the eye, and if she could see it one more time, she might be able to figure out what.

"Okay, if it will set your mind at ease," Decker said. "I'll go down and get it from evidence. You can wait here. There's a coffee machine around the corner, and there might even be a donut or two. We are a police station, after all." He grinned and took a step toward the elevator.

"Stay here? No way. I'm coming with you." Emma hurried to follow.

"I've got this," Decker said. "I'll only be a few minutes. Stay put."

"Not a chance."

"Fine." Decker shrugged. "Are you always this annoying?"

"Nope," Emma replied. "Only when I want to be."

TWENTY-FIVE

DECKER STEPPED INTO THE ELEVATOR, waited for Emma to join him, and then pressed the button for the basement where the evidence locker was housed. The car jerked and started to move, descending downward.

They had barely gone one floor when Decker's phone rang. He looked at the screen. "It's Connor."

"Maybe he found something," Emma said.

"We'll see." Decker answered, putting the phone on speaker.

"John, it's me," Connor's voice filled the elevator car.

"Why aren't you at the precinct?" Decker asked. "You should have waited for me before chasing up a lead."

"I couldn't sleep. Came in early. I had a hunch and wanted to follow it up," Connor said. "It paid off too. I've found something."

"You did?" Decker glanced at Emma. "What have you found?"

"I don't want to tell you over the phone. You have to see this for yourself," Connor replied. "Trust me, it'll be worth it."

"Fine," Decker said. "Tell me where you are."

"An abandoned warehouse in Brooklyn."

"What? Why?"

"I looked into our dead importer, Darzi. He had a second building. He purchased the place years ago to renovate, but apparently never got around to it."

"Really?" Decker raised an eyebrow. "What's the address?"

"1202 Bonham Street."

"Got it."

"Bring the girl too. The archeologist."

"I don't think that's such a good idea."

"We'll need her expertise." The line went silent for a moment. "I'm texting you a photo. Take a look and then tell me we don't need her."

"Hang on." Decker waited while the text came through. When it did, he opened it and stared at the photo Connor had sent. For a moment he was not sure what he was looking at, but then he recognized the strange images - a wall of hieroglyphics.

"Wow." Emma leaned in, looking over Decker's shoulder.

"Do these mean anything to you?" Decker asked her.

"It's hard to say," Emma said. "The picture is so small, but they look similar to the markings we found on the tomb in Thebes."

"You mean the ones chronicling how to resurrect Anubis?"

"Yes." Emma looked worried. "This is huge."

"And there's more too," Connor said. "There are whole walls covered with this stuff. You have got to see it, to believe it."

Emma exchanged a look with Decker. "We have to go down there, right now."

"I thought you wanted to see the statue."

"That can wait. Like you said, it isn't going anywhere." There was a glimmer of excitement in Emma's eyes. "I want to see those hieroglyphics."

TWENTY-SIX

THE SKY HAD GROWN overcast and black by the time Decker and Emma left the precinct house. As they ran to Decker's car and pulled away from the curb, a heavy rain was already falling. The early morning promise of a lovely summer day had turned ominous.

Decker cut through the steady stream of workday traffic. For several minutes they rode in silence. It wasn't until they neared the warehouse address Conner had provided that Emma spoke.

"Listen, about last night." She shifted in her seat and turned toward him.

"What about it?"

"I don't want you to think badly of me." She reached out and touched his arm. "I know it must have put you in an awkward position."

"Not at all." Decker glanced over, his eyes meeting hers for a moment before he focused frontward again.

"I don't make a habit of asking men I barely know to get into bed with me."

"I'm pleased to hear that," Decker said.

"Especially when they are supposed to be protecting me."

"No better place to keep you safe than right there next to you," Decker replied. "Besides, it wasn't exactly a hardship."

"You're so sweet." Emma blushed and looked away. "I don't want to get you in trouble, that's all. It's a strange situation."

"You won't get me into trouble," Decker replied. "I was doing my job, that's all."

"Is that all it was?"

"Sure."

"You climb into bed and cuddle all your witnesses?"

"Not all of them." Decker laughed. "Only the ones I like."

"And how many would that be?"

"Actually, you're the first." They were near the docks now. The city traffic had thinned out. Gone were the yellow cabs transporting tourists around Manhattan, replaced by cargo vans and sixteen wheelers picking up freight from the warehouses that lined the wharfs. A railroad track ran parallel to the road, upon which a train crawled along, pulling boxcars that stretched as far as Decker could see. His eyes wandered over the graffiti that adorned the sides of the carriages, the marks of taggers and vandals from all fifty states now a rolling art show.

"This isn't exactly the best part of town," Emma said as they turned onto Bonham Street. She scanned the large buildings lining the road, most of which had seen better days. Many looked abandoned, their windows long since broken out, more graffiti scrawled across the red brickwork. One was missing part of its roof, twisted girders sagging into the cavernous space within. "It's dreadful."

"Yeah. Criminals rarely pick the best parts of town to house their elicit enterprises." Decker stopped the car and glanced up at the building looming over them, and the faded address stenciled over the entranceway.

1202 Bonham.

"Looks like something out of a horror movie." Emma peered out of the passenger window, a visible shudder running through her.

"You wanted to come." He opened his door and climbed out.

"I know."

"Change your mind?"

"Nope." Emma stood and closed her car door. "Not while I have you to protect me."

TWENTY-SEVEN

THE WAREHOUSE WAS as decrepit on the inside as it was from the pavement. The lobby, or rather, what remained of it, was slowly decomposing, the drywall sagging off the walls to expose the bones of the building. An odor hung in the air, sharp and acidic, masking the subtler reek of decay that permeated the space.

Decker recognized it instantly. Rodent urine.

Emma wrinkled her nose. "Yuck. What is that god-awful smell?"

"Rats," Decker said. "The place is probably infested with them."

"Oh, that's nasty." Emma looked around, as if she expected to find something scurrying toward her. "Where is detective Connor?"

"Your guess is as good as mine," Decker said. "He could be anywhere."

"How are we going to find him?" Emma asked.

Decker was about to reply when a movement off to their left caught his eye. A familiar shape that stepped from the darkness. "I don't think we need to. He already found us."

"John." The shape moved forward, into a beam of slanting light filtered through a tall window facing the street.

Emma turned. "Detective Connor."

"Were you expecting someone else?"

"No." She shook her head. "I was surprised that you weren't outside, that's all."

Connor ignored her. He focused on Decker. "Did you bring any uniforms along?"

"Should we have?" Decker felt a tingle of apprehension.

"No, of course not." Connor glanced around the room. "You want to see the markings?"

"Sure," Decker said. "Lead the way."

Connor motioned for them to fall in behind him. "Keep close and watch your footing There are some rotten floorboards. I'd hate for someone to fall and break their neck." He stepped off into the gloom.

Decker followed.

Emma hesitated a moment, then ran to catch up. She leaned in close to Decker and whispered, "I don't like this place. Maybe we should call in some backup. That is what you guys do, right?"

"And what do I tell dispatch, that we don't like the creepy building?"

"Well, when you put it like that…"

"Are you two talking about me back there?" Connor glanced back over his shoulder.

"Not at all," Decker said. "Where are these hieroglyphics, anyway?"

"It's not far now." Connor led them through a cavernous empty space that fell away in all directions.

Decker could hear the flap of birds in the rafters above their heads. He glanced up but saw only darkness interlaced with the murky outlines of the steel beams that supported the roof. When he looked back down, they were approaching a doorway set into the far wall; the door wedged open on rusty hinges.

"It's in here." Connor paused at the door and stepped aside to allow Decker and Emma to enter first. "After you."

The room beyond was much smaller than the previous one, although it was in a similar state of disrepair. The same odor of feces and urine hung in the air, stronger now that they were in the bowels of the building.

Decker took in his surroundings.

There were several pieces of furniture, each in its own state of decomposition. To their right was an old office desk, the top covered in fallen debris. An executive chair, the fabric long since departed, sat like a strange metal skeleton on the far side of the desk. To the left was another desk. Behind it, a bookshelf sagged under the weight of mold crusted tomes with illegible spines. Deep in the shadows something dripped, a steady tap–tap–tap that added to the gloomy atmosphere.

It took Decker a few moments before his eyes adjusted, bringing more details into focus, and when they did, he took a step backward. They were not alone.

Standing at the far end of the room, watching them, were three figures dressed in black.

Judging from Emma's surprised gasp, she had also noticed the silent trio.

She reached out and clutched Decker's hand. His other hand curled around the hilt of his service revolver.

"I wouldn't do that, if I were you." Connor's voice was low, menacing.

Decker spun around, surprised.

Connor stood blocking the doorway, his gun drawn.

"What are you doing?" A chill ran up Decker's spine.

"Sorry, John." Connor shrugged. He stepped forward and pulled Decker's gun from its holster, then stepped away again. "I wish it hadn't come to this."

"Come to what, Connor?" Decker held Emma's hand tight, reassuring her. "I don't understand."

"If the girl had cooperated, if she hadn't run, everything would be different. You wouldn't need to be here."

"You sent those people to Emma's apartment?" Decker exclaimed, shocked.

"Me? Heavens no." Connor shook his head. "They found me afterward when they realized they couldn't get what they wanted without my help."

"The statue."

"Not only the statue." Connor pointed with the muzzle of his gun. "Her too."

"What?" Decker took a step forward.

"Easy, partner. Don't make me shoot you before I'm ready."

"Okay, okay." Decker backed up. He felt Emma push against him. She was trembling. "How did this happen, Connor?"

"They made me an offer I couldn't refuse. Emma was part of the deal. But she's under your protection, so unfortunately the only way to get her here was to lure you here as well. I thought long and hard about that one, John, I really did. We're more than partners. I've come to think of us as friends."

"I can see that." Decker nodded toward the gun. "Doesn't look like we're friends anymore."

"Sorry, buddy. On the bright side, I'll make sure you die a hero. It's the least I can do, considering the circumstances."

"No one will believe you."

"Yes, they will. They always have. I'm a good liar, John. If only you knew."

"What does that mean?"

"What, you think I could live in this city off a cop's salary?" Connor kept his eyes on Decker. "Don't make me laugh."

"You're on the take."

"Little stuff. Making inconvenient evidence disappear. A false report or two. There are folk in this town that appreciate such things."

"Like who? The Mob?" Decker's mind raced. He wondered if he could reach Connor before the gun went off, if he could disarm him without getting killed. It didn't seem likely.

"Sometimes. But not just organized crime. You'd be surprised at the people who need to make their indiscretions go away. Powerful people. And really, what's the harm? It's not like anyone gets hurt."

"Says the man pointing a loaded gun at his partner."

"Well, I guess I'm moving up in the world."

"What happens now, Connor?" Decker asked. "You shoot us?"

"That would be stupid, wouldn't it?" Connor snorted. "Shooting you with my own service revolver? I bet you'd like that." He stepped forward, his gloved finger flexing on the trigger. "Lucky for me, this isn't my gun. Ballistics will match the bullet to a gang-related homicide last year. As soon as my new friends are finished with the girl, once they have what they want, I'll call it in. Shots fired. Officer down. I'll say we ran into some resistance while investigating this place and that you took a bullet for me, saved my life. At the expense of your own, of course."

"I think I'd figured that much out," Decker replied.

"Enough!" A female voice boomed across the room. The lead figure stepped into the light, and Decker saw that it was a woman with short blond hair, dressed in black from head to toe. She glared at Connor. "Put the gun down."

"What?" Connor froze, a startled look on his face. "Why would I do that?"

"Because I told you to." The figure looked past Connor and nodded.

Connor swiveled, aware a moment too late, that someone had stepped up behind him. The muzzle of a pistol pushed into the back of his neck.

"What are you doing? We had a deal." Connor sounded confused.

"Deal's off. Sorry. Now hand your gun over to my companion."

"This isn't what we agreed," Connor said. "You don't want to do this."

"Oh, but I do."

"You have the girl. I fulfilled my part of the deal."

"Wrong." She shook her head. "I have all of you. The gun. Now."

Connor hesitated, and then, sensing defeat, offered up the revolver.

"And the other one."

Connor handed over Decker's weapon too.

Taking the guns, the man behind Connor spoke for the first time. "I can kill the cops now if you want, Selene. Less to deal with later."

"No. We can't risk drawing attention. First the ceremony, and then we kill them. By that time, it won't matter if anyone hears the gunshots."

"You won't get away with this. I'm a cop." Connor glared at Selene.

"So is he." Selene nodded toward Decker. "And you were about to shoot him."

"But–"

"We're wasting time." Selene motioned to the man behind Connor. "Bring them."

TWENTY-EIGHT

THEY WALKED in silence through the building, weaving through corridors and rooms in varying states of disrepair. Emma kept close to Decker, hugging his side, her hand still gripping his. Connor walked alongside them, his shoulders slouched, head bent low.

Their captors had spread out, two at the front and two at the rear. Selene took the lead position. She glanced back once in a while to make sure everyone was still together.

When she turned, Decker spotted the tattoo on her neck, exactly as Emma had described it, the seated jackal inside an oval. He leaned close and whispered, "Is that the same woman who attacked you?"

"Yes," Emma whispered back.

"What about the others, do you recognize any of them?"

"No, they were wearing masks, remember? I only saw the woman because her mask came off." She paused. "Speaking of which, why aren't they bothering with the masks now?"

"Because they don't care if we see them," Decker said. "They intend to kill us once they get whatever they're after."

"I thought as much." There was a tremble in Emma's voice. "I wonder what they want with me?"

"I don't know," Decker admitted. "I suspect we will find out sooner rather than later."

"That's comforting."

"Sorry." They were coming up to another doorway now. Decker could see two more of the black-garbed figures, one standing on each side of the door. They were herded into the room.

When they entered, Decker could hardly believe what he was seeing. This was nothing like the rest of the decaying building. Here, the floors were swept, and the walls were covered from floor to ceiling in hieroglyphics. Candlelight flickered from dozens of points all around the room, casting long shadows over the space, and illuminating a smooth sandstone bench, above which was a raised dais covered with more carved hieroglyphics. Upon the dais, basking in the soft glow cast by the candles, was something Decker recognized right away.

"Anubis," Emma said.

"No doubt stolen from evidence," Decker said, casting an accusing glance toward Connor.

"Come on, it's just a crappy old statue. What was the harm?" Connor spoke for the first time since becoming a captive.

"Well, for one, you were going to murder us in cold blood," Decker retorted. "Still, it's not all bad. At least when they kill me you will be right there with us. Poetic justice."

"I didn't want to kill you. It was part of the deal."

"How much did they offer you, anyway? What's a life worth these days?"

"Two million." Connor looked down at the floor. "Enough to get out of this job for good and start a new life somewhere else. Guess they won't be paying up."

"My heart bleeds." Decker looked away in disgust.

Connor opened his mouth to reply, but before he could say anything more, a door opened on the far side of the room. One by one, a line of figures entered, each wearing identical black outfits. They filed along, pausing to bow as they passed the statue, before forming a circle around the bench.

The lead figure reached down and brought out a white head-dress adorned with feathers.

Emma let out a gasp. "That's an Atef crown."

"A what?" Decker asked.

"It was the crown worn by priests during certain ceremonies associated with Osiris, god of the underworld."

"I thought you said Anubis was the ruler of the under-world," Decker whispered, confused.

"He was, but at some time before the dawn of the Middle Kingdom, about 2000 years BC, give or take, he was usurped by Osiris."

"Then which one do these nuts worship, Anubis or Osiris?"

"I don't know. Both?" Emma struggled to make sense of what she was seeing. "Maybe they are one and the same god, with a different name. The Egyptians were always changing and combining their deities to suit the times."

"Who cares?" Connor turned to them. "Shouldn't we be looking for a way out of here, instead of having a history lesson?"

"We wouldn't be here at all if it weren't for you," Decker countered.

"We can argue that point later," Connor said.

"Wait." Emma nudged Decker. "Something is going on."

The priest, the man who had donned the headdress moments before, separated himself from the others. He looked their way, his eyes finally settling on Decker and Emma. And then he gestured, speaking in a deep voice.

"The girl." He raised an arm and pointed. "Bring her."

TWENTY-NINE

DECKER STEPPED FORWARD to block the two men as they advanced upon Emma. But before he got far, restraining hands pulled him back. He struggled but to no avail, and he was forced to watch, helpless as Emma was dragged away, a terrified look upon her face.

"Leave her alone." He twisted, trying to break free, an overwhelming sense of dread engulfing him. He had no idea what they were about to do to her, but he knew one thing for sure. Whatever was about to happen couldn't be good.

Emma was near the stone bench now.

They lifted her up and placed her upon it. As they did so, Decker noticed the restraints. There were four of them, two for the ankles, two for the wrists. Emma saw them too. She let out a terrified scream and thrashed wildly, but it was little use, and she was soon tied down.

She turned her head and looked at Decker, eyes wild with fear, but all he could do was watch helplessly while the priest took his place at the foot of the bench. At the other end, the statue towered, dark and insidious.

The woman, Selene, approached the group. In her hands she carried a weighty book with a cracked, stained leather binding. It was old, Decker could tell. Maybe even ancient.

Selene stopped short of the priest.

She offered up the volume with outstretched arms.

The priest opened the book with a gentle reverence, peeling the pages back, one by one, until he reached a point that satisfied him, and then he bowed his head in a silent prayer.

The group moved closer, expectant. They crowded the table, making it hard for Decker to see what was going on.

"Let me go." Emma sounded frantic. "What are you doing?"

The terror in her voice caused a lump to form in Decker's throat. If it weren't for him, she would not be here at all.

"Well, this is odd," Connor said, leaning close to Decker. "I don't suppose you have any brilliant escape plans?"

"Even if I did, they wouldn't include you." Decker never took his eyes from the bench.

"I guess I deserved that," Connor replied. "Still, you know what they say, the enemy of my enemy and all that."

"If we get out of this, I'm going to make sure you spend a very long time behind bars," Decker whispered through clenched teeth.

"Keep it down." Decker's captor twisted his arm. A stab of pain shot up into his shoulder.

"Or what?" Decker retorted.

"Or your death will be long and painful," the man replied. "You should consider yourself lucky."

"Really? Why is that?" Decker asked.

"You'll be one of the few to witness the start of the next great age, to see the release of Anubis from his long slumber."

"You really believe this crap, don't you?" Decker snorted.

"You will too, my friend. Now be quiet. It is beginning."

Decker followed the man's gaze.

The priest lifted his head. He raised his arms. The mood in the room shifted. An expectant silence descended upon the gathered group. All eyes turned to the priest.

Sensing that something was about to happen, Emma cried out, her eyes finding Decker's, a desperate plea contained within the look.

The priest chanted in a language Decker didn't understand, but even to his untrained ear, the words sounded archaic. He had the feeling he was listening to a dialect that had died out alongside the pharaohs.

The black-clad figures huddled around the bench joined in, their voices rising to mix with that of the priest.

Emma tugged at her restraints, wild-eyed. She twisted and thrashed, but her bindings were tight.

The chant reached a crescendo, and as it did, Decker sensed a change in the air. A crackling energy that made the hairs on his arms stand straight.

Then he noticed something else. A growling rumble that pulsed underneath the combined voices of the gathered worshippers. It was faint at first, but building in volume, until it drowned out the chant itself.

Decker winced against the assault on his eardrums, but the group around the bench kept up their strange recital, oblivious to the cacophony of sound.

The chamber grew brighter, illuminated with an iridescence

that overpowered the candles and reached into the very corners of the space.

At first Decker could not identify where the light was coming from, but then he noticed the statue. It glowed as if from some hidden internal illumination. A halo danced around its edges, pulsing ever brighter. He watched, fascinated, as the glow changed from yellow, to orange, to red, and back again, a roiling cauldron of fiery colors within the aura. Finally, as if it had reached tipping point, the light made one last mighty pulse and exploded in a blinding flash; the statue lost in the intense brightness.

"That's some pretty nifty pyrotechnics," Connor said, his voice almost lost in the roaring chant.

Decker ignored him.

A high-pitched scream rose on the charged air, blood curdling and sudden.

Decker knew where it had come from.

Emma.

He forced himself to look past the glare cast by the statue, and what he saw turned his blood cold.

She was still visible, moving in violent fits, her body arching up, and then slamming back down onto the cold, hard table. Her eyes bulged out, and her lips were pulled back in a pained grimace. The scream had died to a guttural moan that was somehow even more frightening.

But that was not all.

The light, which at first seemed to expand in all directions, had focused itself into a throbbing beam that arced from the statue and washed over Emma, surrounding her.

Decker pulled against his captor's grip, desperate to break

free and reach her. But it was useless, and in the end he was forced to stand idle as the light engulfed her.

Moments passed.

The chanting died to a low, mumbling chorus.

Expectant faces watched, waiting.

And then came a sharp snap, followed by another, and two more.

At first the origin of these sounds was not obvious, but soon, rising from the light, Decker saw Emma.

She no longer had a look of pain on her face. Now it was replaced by a countenance of evil. The corners of her lips curled up in a leering sneer that made the gathered throng take a nervous step back. Her gaze swept the room, meeting Decker's for a second, and in that brief exchange he sensed an impossible truth. Behind her eyes lurked a dark, cold presence that had not been there before, and he knew, with absolute certainty, what resided within Emma.

Anubis.

But this was no divine deity. No god reborn to save the believers. It was a thing of pure malice. He had glimpsed that same evil many times when dealing with murderers and abusers. The lowest dregs of human society. But never had he seen so much vile hatred focused in one place—until now. And as he realized this, Decker came to an awful, gut wrenching conclusion.

Emma was gone.

THIRTY

"HOLY SHIT," Connor muttered as the entity that used to be Emma reared up from the arc of light and turned toward the cluster of worshippers. "Are you seeing this?"

Decker didn't bother to respond. His eyes were locked upon the scene unfolding in front of him.

His mind raced.

Nothing made sense. Was there really some dark force inside Emma, controlling her? How could she have broken free of those restraints? It was impossible. But yet, it was real.

Emma, standing atop the bench, turned toward the priest.

He bowed his head, averting his gaze, while a string of mumbled prayers fell from his mouth.

She watched him for a while, and then, in a movement so swift Decker barely registered it, she lunged forward, her arm shooting out, her hand curling around the priest's neck.

He cried out in a hideous, choking gurgle that made Decker shiver.

Emma, or rather the monster that she had become, lifted the priest off his feet. She studied him for a moment and then set him back down upon the floor.

The priest rubbed his neck. "My Lord Anubis, we have awaited your return." His voice was weak, scared.

Anubis spoke in a growling, deep timbre that sounded nothing like the archeologist. "I have looked into your soul and judged you."

"Yes?" The priest looked up, expectant.

"You are not worthy."

"What?" The priest backed away. "But my Lord, I resurrected you."

"I shall judge all who come before me." Anubis stepped toward the priest, one arm outstretched, and made a fist.

The priest let out a cry of pain and clutched his chest, his eyes bugging from their sockets. His face turned crimson, and he struggled to breathe. "Please. It hurts."

"Not worthy." Anubis flicked a wrist.

The priest flew through the air, toppling several of his congregation in the process, and hit the wall where he landed in a crumpled heap.

Decker had no idea what Anubis would do next, and he didn't want to find out.

Neither did the gathering of believers.

In the moments following the attack on their priest, the rest of the worshippers panicked. Terrified, they raced toward the door. Only now there was no orderly line, but instead a thrashing, manic crush to escape.

Anubis turned, and as she did so, the strange light that had enveloped her seemed to glide up her body, curling around her like a serpent, the other end of the coil still attached to the statue.

"None of you are worthy."

She placed her hands together, and when she drew them apart again, a ball of orange fire appeared. She took aim at the fleeing crowd and thrust her hands forward.

The ball shot through the air and parted the desperate escapees like a bowling ball scoring a strike. Bodies flew to the left and right, engulfed in hungry flames, their dying screams dreadful. Then, as quickly as it appeared, the flaming ball ebbed and died.

The crowd at the door, those who had not succumbed to the attack, made one last push to gain freedom. The men restraining Decker and Connor had no desire to stick around for whatever was coming next. They released their captives, backed away, then turned to run.

Anubis had other ideas.

She reached out, targeting the escaping men, and flicked her wrist once more. They took to the air, as if swatted by an unseen hand.

"Holy crap," Connor said. "Did you see that?"

"I guess fleeing is out of the question." Decker looked at Anubis, who had turned her attention toward them.

"Any ideas?" Connor backed up as Anubis stepped down from the bench, the pulsing, coiling light still wrapped around her in a serpentine weave.

"The statue." Decker nodded toward the dais.

"What about it?"

"See how it's still connected to her?"

"So what?"

"I don't think Anubis is entirely free yet," Decker said. "We break that link, we might put an end to this."

"How?"

"You need to distract her." Decker took a step back as Anubis drew closer.

"Why me?"

"Because all of this is your fault." Decker nodded toward the downed guards. He noticed the guns secured in holsters at their hips. "Over there. Go for the guns."

"I'll never make it."

"You don't need to, trust me."

"Shit." Connor hesitated for a moment. "You'd better know what you're doing."

"Do it," snapped Decker.

"Aw, crap." Connor made a sudden move to the left, bolting in the direction of the prone men.

Anubis paused, her gaze fixed on Decker, and then swiveled toward Connor, following him with surprising speed and catching up before he even made it halfway.

Decker wasted no time in rolling to the right, toward the statue.

Behind him, he could hear Connor fighting with the abomination that had once been Emma. He ignored the fracas, not daring to turn and look, hoping that Connor would keep her busy long enough for him to complete his task.

When he reached the dais, Decker grabbed hold of the statue. He ignored the burning agony as he plunged his hands into the strange light.

He grunted and lifted the statue from the dais.

A voice boomed from the other side of the room, deep and commanding. "No."

Decker turned to see Anubis glaring at him through Emma's eyes.

She held Connor by the throat.

He thrashed and struggled.

"What are you doing?" The thing inside Emma screeched. "Put the statue down."

"If you say so." Decker threw the statue with all the strength he could muster.

Anubis cried out and dropped Connor, who crumpled to the floor and lay gasping for breath.

The statue hit the wall with a resounding crash and cracked in half, the ancient ebony splitting from head to toe as it fell to the ground.

The beam of light connecting Emma to the statue recoiled, unwinding itself from her like a wounded snake. The room exploded in a brilliant flash, sending Decker tumbling backwards.

THIRTY-ONE

DECKER LAY ON THE FLOOR, stunned, for what felt like an eternity. He drew in long breaths, every part of his body aching. Finally, with a groan, he struggled up to a sitting position.

The statue of Anubis was broken in two. The strange beam of light had evaporated as if it never existed.

Emma lay sprawled on the other side of the room.

He could not tell if she was alive.

"Emma?" He called out her name.

No answer.

"Speak to me." He wondered what he would do if Anubis was still inside of her. But he knew the ancient god was gone. The air felt lighter than before. Anubis had, it seemed, been dragged back to whatever hell he'd came from. When the statue broke, it had severed the connection.

Decker pulled himself up and staggered toward Emma.

"That's far enough," Connor said behind him.

Decker spun around.

His partner stood several feet away, gun in hand.

"This again?" Decker shook his head. "Don't you think we're a little past that?"

"I can't let you leave, John." Connor's voice sounded rough, forced. "I'm not going to prison over this."

"And you think that killing me is the answer?" Decker replied. He could feel his heart racing. "You won't get away with it."

"We'll see." Connor raised the gun.

Decker saw his finger tense on the trigger.

A shot rang out.

Connor's shoulder whipped back. A spray of blood erupted. He let out a grunt and fell to his knees. The gun slipped from his hand and hit the floor, bouncing away.

Decker turned to see Emma, a pistol in her hand. Their eyes met for a moment. "Is it you in there?"

"Yes, it's me," Emma said. "Whatever that thing was, its gone now." She kept the gun raised.

"I thought you were dead." Decker could hardly contain his relief.

"Nah." She shook her head. "I was out cold for a while though. When I came around, this asshole was about to shoot you." She glared at Connor.

"How did you get the gun?"

She nodded toward one of the two men who had held them captive. "Lucky for us that guy was armed."

"Yeah, lucky." Decker crossed the room and retrieved the other gun. He approached Connor. "Give me a reason."

Connor looked at the gun, then at Emma. "Go to hell."

"Not before you." Decker raised his gun.

"What, you're going to kill me?" Connor said. "Shoot me in cold blood? You don't have the guts."

"You're right, I don't. I have something much worse in mind," Decker replied. "I'm going to put you where you belong, behind bars. Now get up and start walking."

"Where?"

"Outside. As soon as I've got a signal, I'm calling this in. If we're lucky, we might still be able to round up most of the cult members."

"They'll be long gone," Connor said.

"That might be true," Decker glanced around at the injured priest, and those who Anubis had dispatched. "But at least we will have these guys. And you." He glanced over to Emma. "You ready to get out of here?"

"In a heartbeat." Emma lowered her pistol. She crossed the space between them and took his hand in hers. "Let's go."

THIRTY-TWO

DECKER SAT on the tail of an ambulance and waited while the paramedics checked Emma. The parking lot outside of the warehouse was crammed with emergency vehicles, police cars, and a forensics unit. Uniformed officers came and went, dodging in and out of the building. A coroner's van idled close by, back doors wide, waiting to receive those who had not survived the wrath of Anubis. Selene was not among the dead or injured, and that bothered Decker. Several cult members had escaped during the melee, and she was one of them. As for Connor, once he was patched up, he would be on his way to a holding cell on a couple charges of attempted murder, not to mention the corruption charges that were sure to follow.

"Hi."

Decker glanced around, elated to see Emma standing over him. "Are you okay?"

"I'll live." She hopped from the back of the ambulance and put her hand on his shoulder. "Can we go?"

"Sure." He stood and led her to his car, holding the door open. If internal affairs had any questions, they could ask him tomorrow at the precinct. Right now, he was more concerned with Emma than anything else.

He slid into the driver's seat and backing out of the space around a cluster of parked police cars. He edged forward, weaving through the throng of trucks and people until he reached the end of the street.

"Thank you." Emma glanced his way.

"For what?"

"For saving me. For getting me out of there."

"You're welcome." Decker smiled.

They left the warehouse crime scene behind, and headed back toward Decker's apartment, navigating the industrial area's mostly deserted side roads. When they reached a busy intersection, Decker slowed.

He glanced in the rear-view mirror.

To his surprise, a car was coming up behind them, moving much too fast. A sleek black BMW that hurtled along, making no attempt to stop. As the roadster closed in, Decker knew what was about to happen. He lifted his foot from the brake, pushed down on the accelerator, and opened his mouth to warn Emma.

But it was too late.

There was a mighty bang as the BMW barreled into them.

The car lurched forward toward the main road, shunted by the impact. Another second and they would be in the path of oncoming traffic.

Decker turned the wheel hard to the left.

The car slid sideways; the back fishtailing.

Emma let out a terrified scream.

The nose hit the wall of a building and the car came to a juddering stop.

The car might have come to rest, but Decker had not. His body kept going until the seat belt stopped him. His head slammed back into the headrest.

He sat for a moment, stunned.

When he regained his senses and looked at Emma, he was relieved to see that she was still in her seat.

"Are you okay?" he asked.

"I think so," she replied, rubbing her neck. "What the hell was that?"

"We got rear-ended." Decker reached down and unbuckled his seatbelt, then craned his neck toward the BMW.

It sat there; the front crumpled and bent, a wisp of white steam rising from under the hood. But it wasn't the car that drew his gaze. It was the woman dressed in black standing next to it with a gun raised toward them.

Selene.

Decker had barely registered the danger before there was a loud crack. The back window exploded in a spray of glass. A bullet whizzed between them and slammed into the dash.

Emma screamed and ducked down as low as she could.

The gun went off again.

The second bullet opened up a hole in Decker's seat near his shoulder, inches from him. The next one might split his skull.

Decker realized the engine was still running.

He reached down and took hold of the gear stick, slamming it into reverse, and hit the accelerator.

For a moment nothing happened, and he thought that maybe the car was too badly damaged to move. But then, with a shudder, the vehicle sped backwards.

Selene, caught by surprise, barely managed to jump clear, a third shot going wide in the process.

Decker slammed on the brakes, not wishing to hit the opposite wall, and drew his gun.

"What are you doing?" Emma looked terrified.

"Stay here. Keep your head down." Decker threw open his door, flinching as a bullet shattered the wing mirror. He caught a glimpse of movement and squeezed off two rapid shots, then rolled from the car, hitting the ground hard.

He lay there, listening, waiting for the next shot.

It didn't come.

After a while he raised his head and glanced around, but he saw no sign of their attacker. He stood, his gun at the ready, and approached the wrecked BMW.

He stepped to the right, keeping his gun straight ahead, his finger curled on the trigger, but the road was empty.

There was no sign of Selene.

For the second time that day, she had made her escape.

But this time she had not gotten off unscathed. There, on the ground next to the car, was a pool of blood, and leading away, several smaller spatters. She had been shot.

He hesitated, wondering if he should follow. The woman couldn't have gotten far. But he knew he wouldn't find her. She was too smart for that. Besides, he didn't want to leave Emma on her own. He lowered his gun and stood there, gazing down the deserted alleyway until he heard light footsteps coming up behind him. He spun around, bringing the gun to bear until he saw that it was only Emma.

"Easy there." She looked shaken up, with a nasty bruise on her forehead, but otherwise appeared to be fine.

"Sorry." He let the weapon fall to his side.

"She's gone?" Emma drew level and put a hand on his shoulder.

"Yeah," he replied. "I'm afraid so. But not before she took a bullet."

"You got her?"

"Sure did. It must have been a good hit too, judging by all the blood."

"Good." Emma clenched her teeth. "John?"

"Yes?"

"I would really like to get the hell out of here before anyone else tries to kill us."

THIRTY-THREE

TWO WEEKS LATER

DECKER STOOD on the doorstep and rang the bell.

He waited, nervously.

After a while he heard footsteps, and a lock being drawn back. When the door opened, Emma was standing there.

She looked surprised for a moment, and then a smile broke out across her face. "Detective Decker." Her eyes met his. "John."

"Emma."

"I thought you had forgotten about me." She moved aside to let him into the apartment. "It's been so long."

"Sorry about that." Decker looked sheepish. "It's been a busy few weeks with all the questions about what happened in that warehouse."

"Selene?"

"Nowhere to be found." Decker wished he could give her

better news. "We checked all the hospitals, but there was no sign of her."

"Maybe she crawled off somewhere to die."

"Maybe." Decker wasn't convinced. "But to be safe, I've had a patrol car parked up outside to keep an eye on things."

"I saw that. Thank you." She smiled. "And Detective Connor? I assume we don't have to worry about him anymore?"

"He's tucked up in a holding cell awaiting an inquiry by internal affairs, and after that, a trial for attempted murder, among other offences."

"Good."

"The place looks nice," Decker said. "Much better than the last time I was here."

"I had the maid come in." Emma grinned. "Can I get you a cup of coffee, or a cold drink perhaps?"

"No, thank you," Decker said. "I can't stay. I have to be in court in an hour. I was passing and wanted to make sure you were doing okay."

"Oh." The smile waned a little. "I see."

Decker turned toward the door.

"John?"

"Yes?" He turned back to face her.

"What really happened that day?" she asked. "Was I really possessed by Anubis?"

"I don't know," Decker said. "The official story is that we stumbled upon a cult ritual and were all affected by an unknown hallucinogen."

"And all the dead people?"

"They died of heart failure, so it's going down in the books as a mass overdose."

"Is that what you really believe?"

"I have no idea what to believe." Decker shrugged. "At the time I was sure of what I saw, but now..."

"Perhaps it's better to let it go," Emma said. "It'll only drive us mad. Even so, it's a shame the statue was so badly damaged."

"Is it?" Decker replied. "Seems to me that statue was nothing but trouble from the moment you pulled it from the sands. Besides, if an ancient, evil god really was living inside of it, then good riddance."

"I suppose," Emma agreed. "It was magnificent though." She paused. "You really have to go?"

"I do." Decker stepped toward the door, then stopped and looked back at her. "But I'm free tonight."

"You are?" Emma's face lit up.

"Sure." Decker grinned. "You like Italian food?"

"I love it."

"Great. There's a place in Little Italy that will be perfect," Decker said. "The food is amazing."

"Sounds wonderful."

"It is." He looked back over his shoulder and stepped onto the sidewalk. "I'll make reservations and pick you up at eight."

"Okay," Emma agreed. "On one condition."

"Name it."

"We never talk about that damned statue ever again."

The End

Printed in Great Britain
by Amazon

45373667R00086